Midnight Miracle

A REGENCY CHRISTMAS ROMANTASY

Nola Saint James

Pinfeather Press | New York City

For E of M, from whom all blessings flow,
with deepest thanks and gratitude.

For Neil, whose love and support make my work possible.

For Jim/Willie, who keeps my nose to the grindstone
and who loves me.

And a special thank you:
To Shonda Rhimes — for elevating the world of Regency Romance
to new heights, and, in the process,
expanding the possibilities for all of us who spend our days
inhabiting the world of the Regency era.

CONTENTS

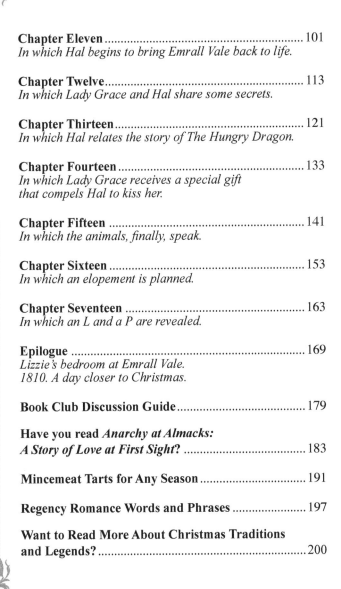

Who is that lovely creature?

WHO'S WHO IN
Midnight Miracle

Our Heroine
Lady Grace Cooper, the orphaned daughter of Viscount and Viscountess Shelbourne, will turn 18 on the last day of December 1804. She has azure-blue eyes and long black curls. Despite her orphaned state, she is happy living in her home, Emrall Vale, a somewhat neglected estate near Symonds Yat, close to the border between England and Wales. She has a kind and loving nature.

Our Hero
Lord Harold (Hal) Neil Picton, 10th earl of Langafel, aka Hal Ravenal, is the son of the 9th earl of Langafel, August Picton, and his wife, Delia Ravenal. She was the daughter of a Roma couple related to the Sinclair family, the Viscounts Ravenscrofft. Orphaned shortly after his birth, Hal was fostered by Alice and Charles Porter, a local couple in the town where he was born. He was unaware of his true heritage until his 18th birthday. He has dark eyes, blue-black hair and a white shock of hair going from his right temple to the base of his skull. This signifies his Roma heritage and his "gift of the horse." Taller than most men, he has an aristocratic nose and supple-looking lips.

Mrs. Beaton, the cook/housekeeper at Emrall Vale. The most recent in a long line of her family to serve the Cooper family. She has been Grace's surrogate mother ever since the death of the girl's parents. She is loving, caring and extremely protective of her charge. She is also the great aunt of Lizzie Hampton, to whom she will read the book, *Midnight Miracle by A Lady in Love.*

Lizzie Hampton, Mrs. Beaton's 15 year-old niece. Lizzie is recovering from a serious illness at Emrall Vale. She has sable braids and grey-green eyes.

Mommia Ravenal, Romany matriarch of the Ravenal clan. A seer and wise woman. Grace's guardian angel.

The Animals
Juno, a calico cat who is a long-time resident of Emrall Vale. Her feline name, unpronounceable by humans, means "Supreme Queen who protects women and children, vanquishes all foes and fights to the death for honor." She considers herself Grace's special protector.

Novo, a small calico cat, full-grown but the size of a kitten, with a black spotted nose. Novo has the ability to sense when the people around her are unhappy. When she picks up a whiff of sadness or discontent, she follows the scent to its source and then applies herself to giving comfort. Her feline name is "She who heals with her purrs."

Mayo is a golden-eyed calico cat who was the companion of the wise woman who lived in the village at the time that The Hungry Dragon tavern got its name.

Blackie, a big, black stallion, a former race horse, Grace's father's mount and the king of the stable. He no longer likes being ridden but he enjoys being turned out in the pasture. He is prone to talking about "shaking" while gazing at Bronwyn with a speculative eye.

Bronwyn, a bay part-Arabian mare, Grace's mother's mount. She will permit Grace to ride her once in a while, but prefers to commune with Blackie in the pasture most days, especially when the weather is warm.

Boy, an aged grey gelding pony and Grace's first mount. He used to pull the pony cart, but feels that he is too old to do so anymore.

Balthazar, a donkey of possible noble lineage. He claims direct descent from Obadiah, the donkey that Jesus rode into Jerusalem. Formerly a companion to Hal Ravenal, but now part of the stable at Emrall Vale.

Supporting Players at Emrall Vale

Miss Harriett Prentice, Grace's very educated but emotionally cold governess

Old Quinn, former stable master/handyman at Emrall Vale.

Young Quinn, Old Quinn's son. The current stable master/handyman at Emrall Vale and Miss Prentice's love interest.

The Villains

The Prospective Bridegroom. Ladies beware!
The 7th Earl of Nottingham, Grace's trustees' choice for a husband. A man who is truly evil, although his razor-sharp aristocratic nose and wavy, gold locks make him very appealing to women, old and young, who don't know any better. His stone-cold, obsidian-black eyes glitter malevolently, especially when he is up to no good. Which is always.

The Trustees – None of whom is to be trusted!
Mr. Grimble, a short, portly man with the face of a weasel. The eldest of the three trustees, he speaks in a high, nasal whine.

Mr. Sykes, a middle-aged, balding man with a grease spot on his cravat that nearly matches a birthmark on his skull. His voice contains an oily wheeze.

Mr. Cranksley, whose girth and height are relatively equal and has nothing else to recommend him.

Novo, a very special feline

PROLOGUE

**Emrall Vale. An estate in the Wye Valley near the border
of England and Wales. 1810.**
*Two weeks before Christmas, in that time when most of the hard
work is done and there's nothing to do but wait.*

Novo, Emrall Vale's resident guardian cat, had a special gift.
The small calico cat always knew when the people around her were
unhappy. When she picked up a whiff of sadness or discontent, she
would follow the scent to its source. Then she would apply herself
to providing comfort. Today, her black spotted nose had led her
to Lizzie, the 15-year-old young lady who was visiting the estate.
She had been very ill, but was now recovering. For the past several
hours, Lizzie had been fussing like a restless kitten. Although she
was better, she wasn't yet well enough to leave her bed. Now Lizzie
was napping. Napping was good. Napping helped one heal.

Novo jumped up onto the Lizzie's bed and made her way to the
pillow. Lizzie seemed agitated, as though troubled by bad thoughts.
The cat assessed the situation, then gently insinuated herself into the
curve between Lizzie's neck and shoulder. Novo began a low, soft
purr. Within a few minutes, Lizzie began to sleep more peacefully.
Novo waved her black, white and ginger tail in triumph. Another
case solved by "She who heals with purrs," her feline name. Then
Novo drifted into sleep herself.

Several hours later.
The first thing that Lizzie Hampton noticed when she woke from
the first sound sleep she'd had in a week, was that there was a small
cat curled up against her neck. The cat had a black spotted nose.
She was purring softly and there seemed to be a slight smile on her
face. Lizzie had never seen a cat smile before. As she observed this
arresting sight, Lizzie's aunt, Mrs. Beaton, entered the room.

"How are you feeling this morning, my dear?" her aunt inquired. "Did you sleep well?" Then Mrs. Beaton noticed the cat and smiled.

"I see that Novo felt you needed her special brand of care," she said. "You must have had a troubled night."

"I had bad dreams, Aunt Beaton," Lizzie said. "And then, suddenly, the bad dreams just went away."

"Novo has a very comforting way about her," said her aunt.

Lizzie sighed.

"I was dreaming about my parents," she said. "It's almost Christmas. We've always been together at Christmas, but this year they're staying with Anne and Charles in Cornwall because the baby is due some time near the end of the year. I was still in school when they left, and they wanted me to finish the term.

"I really appreciate your invitation to stay with you here at Emrall Vale for the holiday season. This is a lovely house. Your employers must think a great deal of you to let you entertain visitors while they're away."

"I've been the housekeeper here for many years, and my aunt before me, said Mrs. Beaton. "The Shelbourne family and my family are distantly related many hundreds of years back. They have always treated me kindly. I raised Lady Grace, the mistress of this house, from the time she was orphaned at five years of age until her marriage.

"She's a countess now," Lizzie's great aunt continued, "married to the Earl of Langafel, a very dear man. This isn't their main estate, but they spend part of the summer and fall here and usually the Christmas season as well. They are glad to have me feel that this is my home.

"Lady Grace is in expectation of a happy event this winter, so they decided to remain in London. If they were in residence, they would have welcomed you and considered you their guest as well as mine."

"I'm glad that at least you and I can be together, said Lizzie, "But I really miss my parents and my sister Anne. Why does she need to have the baby now? Why couldn't she wait until February?"

Mrs. Beaton laughed.

"It doesn't work that way," she said. "Hasn't your mother talked to you about babies?"

Lizzie frowned.

"I asked mama how Anne got with child. She got all red in the face and then said she would explain everything to me on the night before my wedding."

"I can do better than that," said Mrs. Beaton, "when you're feeling a little stronger."

"That would be wonderful," replied Lizzie.

"I'll answer all your questions," continued her aunt, "and I promise not to get red in the face."

"Can't you tell me now?" cajoled Lizzie. "I promise not to get too agitated. I'm so bored."

"I think it would be better for you to be a little stronger before I reveal all the secrets of the marriage bed," replied her aunt with a soft smile.

"The marriage bed? Does that have to do with babies?" Lizzie asked, puzzled. There was a pause. Then she exclaimed, "Oh! Oh my! I never realized …"

"Yes," said her great aunt noting her niece's reaction. "You definitely need to be a little stronger before we discuss the getting of babies. The doctor said that you weren't to get too excited and that you needed to stay in bed for at least another three days."

"But Aunt Beaton," said Lizzie, frustrated, "I'm so bored being in bed. This is a lovely room. It was so kind of you to put me in here. The pink drapes and the matching bed hangings make me feel like a princess. The white and pink-striped cabbage roses on the wall coverings make the whole room feel like a garden. And the portrait of the count and countess keeps me company. It's all so beautiful, but I feel like I need to get out of bed and do something!"

Mrs. Beaton looked at her beloved great niece, whose sable braids lay damp and disordered on the bolster beneath her head. Her grey-green eyes, so like her mother's, lacked their usual sparkle. Mrs. Beaton was so glad to have her great niece's company. Truth to tell, she had been feeling a little lonely herself and had been looking forward to Lizzie's visit to Emrall Vale. Then, barely a week after Lizzie had arrived, she had fallen ill with a virulent fever that had swept through the area.

Thanks to the combined skills of a local Romany healer, a friend of Mrs. Beaton's, and the local doctor, no one in the area had died. It had been, though, a very near thing with Lizzie. The dear girl had been happy and energetic one day and hovering on the brink of death the next.

"I know, my dear, said Mrs. Beaton to Lizzie. "You've had a difficult time of it. But the doctor and the healer all agreed that you need to stay in bed and rest a few more days. After all, you don't want to fall ill again."

"It's just that I was so sick and now I'm feeling so much better," said Lizzie. "I know that I'm not really strong enough to get out of bed and do things, but I can't help wanting to! If I could read, I'd be fine. But I tried reading yesterday and it gave me a terrible headache. It's almost Christmas and I want to feel well again!"

Mrs. Beaton thought for a moment and then said, "If you can't read, I'll read to you. And I know just the book that will make you feel better!"

"I guess that would be better than just lying in bed staring at the canopy of the bed hangings," responded Lizzie somewhat ungraciously.

Her great aunt smiled. Lizzie was always charming and polite. Too polite, in Mrs. Beaton's opinion. Perhaps there would be some positive outcomes from this illness.

"I'll go get the book," said Mrs. Beaton, rising.

There was silence for a moment and then Lizzie asked, "What is it about?"

Curiosity, thought Mrs. Beaton. Another good sign.

"It's a story about a Christmas miracle and true love," she replied.

"A Christmas miracle and true love," sighed Lizzie. She was beginning to think about becoming a woman and falling in love and marrying, just like her parents. They seemed so happy together. She smiled.

"That sounds absolutely lovely," she said and yawned. "Maybe I'll just take a little nap first. She closed her eyes and fell into a deep sleep. Novo's soft purring song accompanied her into sweet dreams.

Some hours later, Lizzie was awake and alert. She was excited to hear her great aunt read to her. She remembered a time when she was little. Mrs. Beaton had visited her and had read to her then. Lizzie recalled that the older woman liked to act out all the parts of a story. She smiled.

Mrs. Beaton pulled a well-upholstered chair up to the side of Lizzie's bed. A cloud-soft, moss-green shawl was wrapped around her shoulders. The fire in the fireplace had been built up so that the room was quite warm. There was a cup of tea on a small table next to her.

"Now then," she said. "Are you ready to hear a story of true love?"

"Oh yes!" responded Lizzie.

Mrs. Beaton opened the book and cleared her throat. Lizzie saw that the book was bound in rose-colored, watered silk and that the pages had gold edges. It was a beautiful volume, she thought. She wondered where her aunt had found it. Her aunt began to read.

"Midnight Miracle," her aunt said, "by a Lady in Love. Chapter One."

The Earl of Nottingham

CHAPTER ONE
*In which an evil plan
is put in play.*

Emrall Vale. August, 1804.

"Not much of an incentive you're giving me, gentlemen," said the 7th Earl of Nottingham. He turned to the three elderly men. They had invited him to this desolate corner of rural England. He surveyed the obviously long-neglected property with disdain.

Messrs Grimble, Sykes and Cranksley were the trustees for orphaned Lady Grace Cooper, the young heiress to the property. The four men stood outside the door of the sagging stable and watched a couple of old horses and an even older pony cropping grass in the paddock. The fences were in need of mending, the earl noted.

"You want me to marry a chit not yet out of the schoolroom with nothing to recommend her? And, you expect me to share her dowry with you? As Miss Grace Cooper's trustees," said the earl, "I would think that you would offer more of an inducement to me for helping you embezzle her funds. At the very least, you ought to provide me with something I don't already have.

"I've already got one down-at-the-heels estate in Ireland. I certainly don't need another in the middle of nowhere. Close to the border of Wales, no less," he muttered. He sneered, looking down his razor-sharp nose at the three gentlemen who had been following him around the Emrall Vale estate for the last hour.

The most senior of the trustees, Mr. Grimble, protested. The earl thought that Grimble, a short, portly man, had the face of a weasel.

"Really, my lord," said Grimble in a high whine. "Embezzle is such an ugly word. It's not a matter of embezzlement at all! We wish to do you a good turn."

"No, no, it's really not, not at all," chimed in Sykes.

Looking down at the man, the earl noticed that Sykes had a grease spot on his cravat that was similar in shape to the large red birthmark on his balding pate.

Grimble continued.

"Why, there's no embezzlement at all! It's just a matter of our being paid for taking care of the young lady all these many years. Surely the hours and hours we've spent managing the estate and its finances should be compensated. It's only right, only right," he said, his head bobbing up and down.

"Indeed," added Cranksley, whose short stature and wide girth, the earl noted, were equal, giving the impression that he might fall over and roll away at any minute. "There was no provision in the will for payment of the trustees. It's a great deal of work, taking care of an estate this size, as well as all the staff and the orphan girl. Girls are so very difficult, you know."

"I don't see any staff," responded the earl, interrupting the trustees. Where are they?"

"Had to let most of them go, didn't we?" whined Grimble. "A huge financial drain on the estate. Only the girl and the housekeeper live here. Why should we pay for footmen and maids and gardeners and such? A waste of money."

"No, no, it's really not, not at all," said Sykes.

"The stable master takes care of the horses and the pony. Worthless animals, but when we made plans to sell them, the girl kicked up such a fuss that we let her have her way. To save money, we fired the last footman and told the stable master to take care of repairs around the place," explained Grimble.

"There's a governess, of course" interjected Cranksley. "It wouldn't be proper for a viscount's daughter not to have a governess. We found an impoverished baron's daughter for the role. Good bloodlines but nothing to look at."

"No, no, it's really not, not at all.

"Skinny and cold," the earl heard Cranksley mutter. So, the man had made advances and been rebuffed, thought the earl. He shook his head. Cranksley was hardly a young girl's dream. Well, it wasn't his business. The earl's thoughts went back to the comment about the girl's reaction to the proposed sale of the animals.

"Is the girl difficult?" asked the earl in a menacing tone. "The very last thing I want t is a difficult maiden. It's not that I can't handle such a girl, but it's such a bother and a bore."

"No, no, it's really not, not at all," Sykes almost shouted.

"She's not difficult at all!" said Grimble. "That was quite some time ago. She was a youngster then. You know how girls are. They get to that terrible stage. Everything is cause for a fight. Not yet a young woman and no longer a girl. They can be hot-headed for a while, but then they settle down and prepare to be good wives and mothers."

"Exemplary wives and mothers," mumbled Cranksley, nodding in agreement. "Lady Grace is everything that she should be."

"Lovely chit," said Grimble.

"Nice figure," concluded Cranksley.

The earl thought he heard Sykes mutter, "yes," but it was so soft an exhalation that he couldn't be sure.

Grimble cleared his throat.

"To get back to the issue of our financial claim on the estate," he said. "The first year, we realized there was no arrangement for compensating the trustees. We three convened a meeting with the lawyer of the estate to discuss the issue."

"No, no, it's really not, not at all," asserted Sykes.

"Notes were taken, as was right and proper," added Grimble.

"We all agreed that there should be a letter added to the will putting forward a reasonable amount of compensation for our work," Cranksley said. "Mr. Runsee, the solicitor, who had been the family's man of business for many years, went off to draw up the papers."

"It was the dead of winter," said Grimble. "The streets in London were sheets of ice."

"Walking up the stairs to his chambers, his foot slipped," continued Cranksley. "Runsee fell and cracked his head against the paving stones."

Grimble shook his head in a pantomime of sorrow.

"A shame", said Grimble. "A life cut short at 89. Poor soul, in the prime of life."

"And there was no other solicitor to take his place, you see," explained Cranksley. "When we heard of Runsee's death, we had another meeting. We decided that it was up to us to appoint a solicitor for the estate. My sister's nephew's son had just completed his apprenticeship. We offered him the position of solicitor to the estate, and he was happy to get it, times being hard just then."

Conscientious young man," said Cranksley. "Quite diligent."

"We set him up in very nice chambers," said Grimble. "Right next to our suite. We're his only client. He takes very good care of us."

"So you see, my lord," said Cranksley, "everything is all right and proper as it should be. An agreement to share Lady Cooper's dowry equally is a very efficient method for the trustees to be paid for our work."

"All we need to do is agree on the details before you marry her," clarified Grimble. "The marriage contracts and all."

"Nothing at all shifty about it," muttered Cranksley.

"No, no, it's really not, not at all," said Sykes.

"I see," said the earl.

And he did see. He sighed. He so disliked dealing with petty criminals. They were usually both venal and incompetent. It was a bad mix. The earl much preferred working with men who knew their business. Professionals. Much less complicated and straight forward. However, the chance to take over this potentially very lovely estate and to get a young wife into the bargain had been more temptation than he could resist. He wouldn't make it easy for the trustees, however.

The earl sighed and ran his fingers through his sun-streaked gold locks. Women loved to play with his hair. He looked around. Where was the heiress? He had been told that she never left the estate except to go to church. Shouldn't she be around somewhere? Her absence was odd. He didn't like things that were odd.

The earl didn't really care to meet this Grace person before he married her. On the other hand, if he spied her wandering about, perhaps he might steal a kiss or two. She wouldn't have to know that he was to be her bridegroom. Wouldn't she be surprised when they stood in front of the priest in St George's Church, to see who she was marrying! After he finished these negotiations, he would wander around the estate by himself. Sometimes luck favored the bold.

"My lord?"

It was Grimble, asking for his attention. The earl sighed. Best to get the details settled. The earl looked at the trustees. His cold, obsidian-black eyes glittered malevolently in the sunlight. More astute men than these three would have seen that look and given their scheme up for a bad job.

"Amateurs!" reflected the earl. Was it really worth dealing with them? In that moment, he decided that what the trustees had proposed just wouldn't do. He would have to append a nuisance tax to the transaction or he just wouldn't be happy with this day's work.

"I want three-quarters of the dowry," the earl said. "When you told me about this estate, you said that it was in good repair. Instead, I find a house that's practically falling down and a stable and outbuildings that won't last another winter. The whole place should be burned to the ground. Better just to start fresh, I think. When I take charge, that's what I shall do. One good spark should be sufficient."

"Burned to the ground?" exclaimed Grimble. "This property has been in the Cooper family for over 300 years! We thought you would want to live here with your new wife."

"Live here?" The earl glared at the three men as though they had lost their wits. "I live in London! In Mayfair! I plan to bring my new wife to my estate in Ireland and leave her there, just as I did with her predecessor."

"Died in childbirth. God rest her soul. My condolences, my lord," muttered Cranksley.

"I will make certain that my new wife is well on her way to birthing my heir before I return to London," the earl continued, ignoring Cranksley's remark. "If she doesn't produce my heir, I'll visit her in Ireland and stay with her until she does. She and the child will enjoy the fresh Irish country air.

"This place is criminally neglected! There's no staff to speak of other than a governess, a stable master — not even a groom — and a cook," continued the earl. "The work of staffing such an estate here, in the middle of nowhere, is not to be thought of. Besides, if I don't burn this place down, it will cost thousands to put the property to rights so that it can be sold."

"No, no, it's really not, not at all. Sold?" exclaimed Sykes.

The earl turned away and let the silence expand. He heard the men shuffling their feet and speaking to one another in low whispers. He waited.

"My lord," Grimble said hesitantly. The earl pretended not to hear him.

"My lord." Grimble spoke again, slightly louder. The earl turned slowly toward him and raised his left eyebrow, while looking down his nose.

Grimble cleared his throat.

"You can, of course, do whatever you wish with the estate once it is yours," the man said, deferentially.

"Indeed," chimed in Cranksley. "No restraints on your actions at all. The place is not entailed."

"No, no, it's really not, not at all," added Sykes.

"Please, my lord," said Grimble obsequiously, "perhaps you would like to view the interior of the manor house? The rooms are quite pleasantly proportioned."

"And the kitchen is almost modern," added Cranksley.

"The housekeeper, Mrs. Beaton, is an excellent baker, especially her muffins and her raisin scones," added Grimble.

The earl examined each of the conspirators in turn, his face devoid of any emotion. Then he took a deep breath.

"I've seen all I need to see. Let's go take care of the paperwork. Then I'm off to London. I want this matter completed with all due haste," he said. "I shall obtain a special license at the estate's expense," he added, narrowing his eyes and looking at the trustees as though challenging them to object. None of the men objected. "I want my bride wedded and bedded on the first of the year."

"I need to get my hands on her dowry as quickly as possible," thought the earl. "My creditors are getting impatient. If I throw them a few pounds and tell them of my expectations, they will surely be willing to wait for a while."

The earl drew himself up to his full height and glared down at the three men. He exuded four hundred years of aristocratic breeding and entitlement.

"You will also give me oh, let's say, a thousand pounds, within the next week to guarantee this transaction," he said.

The trustees looked at one another, stunned. This had not been in their plans. Their cash reserves were somewhat depleted at the moment, having borrowed liberally from Lady Grace's income for their own plans for the upcoming holiday.

"No, no, it's really not, not at all. Not possible," said Sykes.

"So much to arrange, after all, said Cranksley."

"Surely, for earnest payment," said Grimble, "a sovereign would do."

"Quite right, quite right, said Cranksley, "a sovereign." Looking up into the earl's face and noticing his scowl, Cranksley added, "or perhaps two?"

"Your reticence to be forthcoming with a respectable earnest payment makes me wonder if you have been playing ducks and drakes with the young lady's income," said the earl. "Three quarters of nothing is nothing. I begin to suspect that you three are wasting my time."

Turning away from the men, the earl began to walk toward his carriage.

""No, no, it's really not, not at all," said Sykes.

"Everything is in order, my lord," said Grimble.

"Yes, yes, my lord," Cranksley assured the irritated aristocrat.

They all hurried after the earl, whispering to one another as they went.

"Good!" thought the earl. "Now I've set the cat among the pigeons." Just before reaching his carriage, he turned and faced the trustees.

"Well?" he asked.

Cranksley thought that he had never heard a man sound both bored and irritated at the same time.

"No, no, it's really not, not at all," said Sykes.

 "Surely we can work something out, said Grimble."

Sykes and Cranksley nodded their heads in agreement.

"You have vexed me exceedingly," said the earl, "for which you must pay. You will deliver three thousand pounds to me in London by the time I leave for my club tomorrow evening or there is no agreement."

"No, no, it's really not, not at all," said Sykes.

"Not a problem at all, my lord," said Cranksley.

"All will be done as you wish, my lord," chimed in Grimble.

"Three thousand, yes of course, my lord. A very fair sum, very fair," mumbled Cranksley.

"There is one other thing, my lord," said Grimble.

The earl narrowed his eyes and stared at the trustee. Didn't these men know when to slink away and get about their business? he wondered.

"What?"

The word was a staccato utterance.

Deferentially, Grimble said, "Don't you wish to meet your prospective bride? The housekeeper says that she's away visiting friends, but we can surely hunt her down and bring her to meet you here in a day or so."

"Why would I wish to meet her?" asked the earl, sounding bored. "Women are interchangeable. You've told me that she's acceptable. I take your word for it. No need to meet her before the wedding.

"You will send a carriage to bring her to London so that she will arrive on the last day of the year, the earl continued. "I will arrange for her to stay with one of my female relatives for the night. If I am going to bring this place up to snuff just enough to sell it, rather than incinerate it, I will need three-quarters of my little wife's dowry. Take it or leave it. I'm a busy man. We've been out here in nature so long I feel my shins growing moss!"

"But my lord," said Cranksley. Grimble shoved his elbow into his fellow trustee's ribs to silence him.

"No, no, it's really not, not at all," stammered Sykes.

"Let us retire to the inn where we left our belongings," suggested Grimble. "After dinner ..." he paused. The earl had a grim look on his face. "Or before, if you prefer, my lord, we can draw up our agreement and be gone in the morning."

The Earl of Nottingham surveyed his new property. Of course he wouldn't burn it down. Or sell it. Perhaps he would settle several of his young wards in the house and use the property as an occasional respite from London. When he had his little wife's dowry, all his money problems would be solved. Then he could relax. He licked his lips and turned back toward his carriage. Yes, this estate would suit him very well. Very well indeed.

Juno – Protector of Emrall Vale

CHAPTER TWO
In which we learn that Lady Grace has many protectors.

Juno, a large orange calico cat of uncertain age, ruled the stable, the house and all she surveyed at Emrall Vale. She had been napping in the sun in her favorite corner of the barn. Her black ears pricked forward when four men approached the stable. They smelled wrong. Why had they invaded her domain?

Juno understood the words of humans. She had done so since she was a kitten, many, many seasons ago. She had come to learn that not all cats could follow human conversation, although most could understand words like food, bed and warm. She, however, understood everything that they said. This had led to her extreme longevity. She could hear trouble coming and would make herself scarce until the trouble had passed.

Juno disliked men on general principle. They rarely gave her treats and felt that, especially in the drawing room, they had the right to sit anywhere they wished. They did not acknowledge the established order of the universe in which cats ruled.

She could also communicate with other animals. The two horses and the pony in the Emrall Vale stable were quite pleasant company. They were interesting to speak with on a long winter's night. Right now they were idling in the paddock, but she knew that they were also listening to the conversation of the four men.

All the animals on the estate shared a common purpose — to keep the young mistress safe. The young mistress had been left an orphan when she was only five years old. Such a youngling needed protection. Juno and the horses, Blackie, the stallion, Bronwyn, the bay mare and Boy, the steel-grey gelding pony, all understood what could happen to a young thing that was left alone in the world.

The day they heard that her parents would not be returning to Emrall Vale, all the animals made a pact to protect her as best as they could. The cook, who lived in the big house, was also a watchkeeper. It was sometimes helpful to have a two-legged in the vicinity.

Juno had few memories of her early life, but she remembered they called her Juno because she had been born in June. Of course, Juno had a secret feline name. It was only known to other cats and was unpronounceable in the human tongue. It meant "Supreme Queen who protects women and children, vanquishes all foes and fights to the death for honor."

Juno knew she didn't like the young, gold-haired man. He had the worst smell of the four men — like something acrid and decaying. She listened as the men spoke and understood that they were going to take the young miss away from Emrall Vale. Juno was determined that she would thwart this evil plan. This very night, she would confer with her stablemates. They would all come up with a plan to keep their girl safe from harm.

Mrs. Beaton, the cook and housekeeper at Emrall Vale, had been with the family even before her young mistress, Lady Grace Cooper, had been born. Mrs. Beaton's family had been in service to the Cooper family for generations. Ever since Grace's parents, Viscount and Viscountess Shelbourn had died in a carriage accident, Mrs. Beaton had taken the young, orphaned girl under her wing and considered herself Grace's surrogate mother as well as the estate's housekeeper and cook.

She had a cozy suite of rooms off the kitchen. Her bedroom had its own fireplace, but she only used the fireplace during the coldest winter days. The kitchen fireplace generated enough heat to warm both her bedroom and the kitchen. A dressing room adjoined the bedroom. Besides room for her limited wardrobe, the room featured a simple washstand and a dressing table with a small mirror. A large trunk, where Mrs. Beaton kept her most prized possessions, stood in one corner.

On the dressing table was a set of silver-backed hair brushes and a small box that held a broach, a gift from Grace's mother. A water closet could be entered from the dressing room.

Next to Mrs. Beaton's bedroom was the housekeeper's parlor. A large desk commanded the room. On it were stacked the housekeeping accounts, a few bills and a writing set consisting of a crystal ink well with a silver top, a silver letter opener and a folding pen knife with a worked silver case. These had been a gift from Mrs. Beaton's aunt when Mrs. Beaton had come to Emrall Vale to take her place. At the time, her aunt had explained that the set had been handed down from one housekeeper at Emrall Vale to another for several hundred years.

Mrs. Beaton was very satisfied with her accommodations at Emrall Vale and was happy to be in such a comfortable position.

And, never married or with children of her own, she was delighted when Grace was born. She always devoted a few minutes in every day to visit the young child in the nursery. Mrs. Beaton grew to love the little girl.

While Grace's parents lived, they educated her themselves. Although she was very young, Grace quickly learned to read and to do simple arithmetic. For her third birthday, her parents gave her a blue leather-bound journal. They had ordered it for her from a bookbinder in London. The journal had a title, The Daily Adventures of Lady Grace Cooper, stamped on the cover in gold.

Grace's parents suggested that Grace draw pictures in her journal every evening so she could remember each day. When she learned to write, they told her, she could write about all her adventures and also draw pictures.

Grace was thrilled with her journal. She knew that her parents loved books. They had given her a book with her very own name on it! Grace drew her first picture that night. It showed a young girl being given a blue book with gold writing on it by a man and a woman.

Every evening, right before saying her prayers, Grace would record her thoughts and feelings in her journal, at first through pictures and then, as she matured, in words as well. For Christmas, the year after her parents died, Mrs. Beaton gave Grace a new blue leather-bound journal just like the one her parents had given her.

"Your parents would want you to continue to write and draw," Mrs. Beaton told Grace. "When you write in your journal at night, perhaps you will feel like you are telling your parents about your day. That way, you will always feel close to them."

Grace had cried, and then hugged Mrs. Beaton with all her might. And she followed her friend's advice.

Life at Emrall Vale had changed when Grace's parents died. Grace's trustees dismissed her nursery maid and the cook, to save money, they said. They explained to Mrs. Beaton that the estate's income was strained to the limit and asked her to take on the role of cook. They also charged her with Grace's upbringing.

Mrs. Beaton agreed to take on the additional responsibilities for Grace's sake. However, she told the trustees that Grace must have a governess to educate her as was appropriate for a viscount's daughter.

The trustees initially rejected the need for this expense, but Mrs. Beaton persisted. She had the local vicar write to them about the education that Grace's parents would want for their daughter. In the end, they relented.

The governess the trustees engaged for Grace, Miss Prentice, was a cold, reserved woman, but she was extremely well educated. In addition, she was the granddaughter of a baron who had fallen on hard times. The trustees believed that, when the time came, Miss Prentice could teach Grace to conduct herself with the propriety demanded of a daughter of a viscount.

Miss Prentice gave Grace a solid foundation in literature, mathematics, natural history, French drawing room conversation, music and sketching. She even taught her a little of the classics: Latin, Greek and Hebrew, the better to study her bible. What Miss Prentice did not give Grace, was affection.

Early on, Mrs. Beaton realized that if her young charge was to have love in her life, she would have to provide it. Mrs. Beaton and Miss Prentice had come to an agreement. The governess would tutor Grace for five hours in the morning and then have the rest of the day to herself. Grace would take her meals in the kitchen with Mrs. Beaton rather than alone in the nursery. In addition, Mrs. Beaton would keep an eye on Grace when she wasn't in her lessons.

The trustees didn't care how the household was run. As long as Mrs. Beaton managed with the small quarterly allowance they gave her, they didn't interfere. The arrangement seemed to satisfy everyone.

Over time, the trustees dismissed the remaining footmen and maids, citing the need to economize. By the time Grace was eight years old, the only staff other than Mrs. Beaton and Miss Prentice was Young Quinn, the stable master.

Young Quinn was the son of Old Quinn. Old Quinn had served as stable master at Emrall Vale since Grace's father was a boy. Young Quinn had started working in the stables at Emrall Vale when he was a teenager. He had taken over the job from his father about a year after Grace's parents died.

Young Quinn had proved to be an adequate addition to the staff. Besides taking care of the two horses and the pony, he chopped wood for the house, fixed the fencing when absolutely necessary and did some light gardening. If he wasn't the most hard-working of men, at least he took excellent care of the animals in the stable.

Young Quinn lived at home with his retired father and came to Emrall Vale every morning.

The year that Grace turned 17, Mrs. Beaton noticed that Young Quinn, who was in his mid-twenties had been spending more and more time in the afternoon talking with Miss Prentice. Miss Prentice began taking Sunday dinner with the Quinn family. Mrs. Beaton watched this courtship with interest.

The housekeeper believed that young people needed a lot of exercise and fresh air. She encouraged Grace to play outside as much as possible. Grace loved the freedom of wandering around the Emrall Vale estate and learning about the plants and animals that flourished there.

No matter how long Grace had been outside, every day she made time to spend at least a few minutes in Mrs. Beaton's parlor. She would curl up in the room's cozy sofa and gaze at the wedding picture of her parents.

The portrait, which had hung in the rarely used formal receiving room while Grace's parents had been in residence, was moved to Mrs. Beaton's parlor after their death. It had pride of place over the fireplace opposite her desk. Grace loved to look at it while Mrs. Beaton told her stories about her parents.

Every once in a while, Miss Prentice would object to the amount of time that Grace spent outdoors. If Grace was allowed to roam the countryside, she would tell Mrs. Beaton, the girl would turn into a heathen. Grace would never develop the demure attitude necessary for her to become a true lady.

Mrs. Beaton would remind Miss Prentice of their agreement. That was usually the end of the discussion, at least for a time. To provoke the governess, Mrs. Beaton would then encourage Grace to spend even more time outside having fun.

On one such adventure, when she was about eight years old, Grace met a friendly Romany woman and they had fallen into conversation. Mommia — she pronounced it moh-ME-ah — was a woman who seemed to be about the same age as Mrs. Beaton.

Mommia had shown Grace a fox's den and had explained that the mother and father foxes raised their kits together. That's why, Mommia had said, it was cruel to hunt foxes. If a fox was killed, its mate would have to raise the kits alone. There was a good chance that some of them would die because one fox couldn't guard the den and hunt for food at the same time. On the neighboring estate, Ravens Keep, where Mommia and her clan lived, fox hunting was not permitted for this reason.

Thinking about orphaned fox kits made Grace cry. Mommia gathered her into a warm embrace and held her until her crying stopped. She rocked Grace back and forth, singing a wordless song. Grace felt safe. Mommia didn't ask Grace why she was crying. She seemed to know. She gave Grace a large handkerchief and helped her dry her eyes.

"Now, my little kit," said Mommia. "You'll be just fine. Your mama and your papa are watching over you in heaven and they love you. Mrs. Beaton loves you. All the animals at Emrall Vale love you. And if you permit it, I will love you as well. One day, when you are grown, you will meet a wonderful man and he will love you and give you children of your own to love. He'll be the love of your heart."

"But Mommia," Grace had asked, "how will I know that the man is the love of my heart?"

"When the time comes, you will know," said Mommia. "In the meantime, I will come to you when you wander in the woods, and I will teach you all about this beautiful world."

"I would like that very much," said Grace.

Mommia had walked her to the edge of the forest. She watched as a large calico cat with black ears and a white tail came out of the stable to greet her. Grace bent down to scratch the cat behind the ears. The cat rubbed her head against Grace's hand. Mommia smiled. Her little kit had a lot of guardians.

About once a year, the trustees paid a visit to Emrall Vale, purportedly to check on Grace's welfare. They always sent Mrs. Beaton a note well in advance. Mr. Grimble always added a personal note to say that, should Mrs. Beaton care to serve them her famous muffins with elderberry jam for tea, he would be most grateful.

Mrs. Beaton wasn't completely dependent upon the trustees for information about their plans for Grace. Through a friend's son who worked in the trustees' office, she had discovered that the trustees planned to arrange a marriage for Grace. The marriage would permit the three men to benefit financially.

Grace was a considerable heiress. However, she did not have access to her funds because she was a minor. She lived by the whims of her trustees until she was 21. By then, they would have married her off and her husband would control her fortune.

In the early morning hours of the day when the trustees were expected to visit, Mrs. Beaton was abruptly awakened by a terrifying dream. For a few moments, she didn't know where she was. All she could think about was the vision in her dream of a golden-furred wolf with gleaming red eyes. He and three snarling weasels were charging towards Emrall Vale. Mrs. Beaton shivered violently. The dream felt so real. What could it mean?

Unwilling to go back to sleep lest the dream return, Mrs. Beaton dressed and went down to the kitchen to begin her bread baking. As she worked, the feeling of menace that had been so vivid in the dream, seemed to grow. It was almost as though evil was coming closer and closer to Emrall Vale.

Unable to throw off the feeling of menace, Mrs. Beaton hurried to Grace's room to make sure her girl was safe. She noticed that Juno was following her. As she opened the bedroom door, the housekeeper noticed how neat and clean the room was. This was always the case. With no housemaids, Grace had to look after her own things and keep her bedroom tidy. This was unusual for a titled young lady, but Grace never complained. "She is such a good girl," Mrs. Beaton thought.

Mrs. Beaton parted the blue velvet hangings on the bed that Grace had closed to keep warm. The girl was sound asleep. Under her head was a blue silk kerchief that had belonged to her mother. Mrs. Beaton knew that Grace had slept with the kerchief every night since her mother's death almost 13 years before.

The housekeeper looked down at her charge. Why did she feel

that her dream was a warning about harm that might come to Grace? The girl might be safe now, but Mrs. Beaton wasn't taking any chances. Grace would be 18 on the last day of this year. As that date drew closer, Mrs. Beaton feared that the trustees would scheme to marry Grace to any man they chose. The housekeeper was determined that wouldn't happen. She shook Grace awake.

"What's wrong?" asked Grace.

"I've had one of my dreams," said Mrs. Beaton.

"Oh!" exclaimed Grace. She knew, from prior experience, that Mrs. Beaton's dreams were not to be ignored. Mrs. Beaton had told her, just a few years before, that the morning that Grace's parents had left on their doomed trip, Mrs. Beaton had dreamed of a carriage accident. Grace respected Mrs. Beaton's abilities as a seer.

"Get dressed as quickly as possible," said Mrs. Beaton. "Then come down to the kitchen to break your fast. I'll make you some sandwiches and a flask of lemonade. Go into the forest and stay far away from the house. When it's safe, I'll send Juno to find you."

Grace immediately got out of bed and went to make her morning ablutions. She pulled out a sturdy dress and her half boots. She had long ago assembled what she thought of as a uniform for wandering in the woods.

Over a greyish-brown dress, she wore a soft leather apron with a number of pockets. In the pockets were all types of implements that Grace might need on her rambles — a ball of heavy string, a small pair of scissors, tweezers, a needle and a spool of thread, several buttons, a length of ribbon and a few hair pins. One special pocket was deep enough to hold a sandwich and an apple. There was even a leather loop with which she could attach a covered jar of lemonade. All in all, it was a very useful garment.

Dressed for her day in the woods, Grace looked much younger than her almost 18 years. She grabbed a large straw hat and a light shawl — it was sometimes cool in the forest — and hurried down to the kitchen.

Mrs. Beaton had prepared some porridge with summer fruit for her, several slices of toast spread with butter, sugar and cinnamon and a cup of tea. The food was set on the long wooden table in the center of the cozy kitchen. Grace hurried over to the table. She offered thanks for her meal, as Mrs. Beaton had taught her to do, and then began to eat. She was looking forward to her ramble in the woods. But at the same time, she wondered what terrible thing Mrs. Beaton had seen in her dream …

The ancient apple peel ritual

CHAPTER THREE
In which Lady Grace performs the apple peel ritual.

September.

It was a crisp fall day. Grace sat at the wooden table in the kitchen, a basket of Ashmead's Kernel apples from the orchard in front of her. She methodically worked the fruit so that the golden-brown peel stayed in one piece. As she cut into the cream-yellow flesh of the fruit, a tart, citrus-like aroma was released. A pile of peels sat discarded next to her. She performed this ritual every month.

"When you're finished, I'll use the apples and the peels for a crumble," Mrs. Beaton said to Grace, leaning forward to take the completely peeled fruit from the girl's hand. Grace retained the apple peel, peering at it thoughtfully.

"I suppose that this is as good a peel as I'm going to produce," she said.

"Then go on with your ritual," sighed Mrs. Beaton, a resigned smile on her lightly lined face. "Don't know as it will give you any better results than the last hundred times you performed it."

Grace laughed.

"I haven't done this ritual a hundred times," she protested. "But I must find my true love! I'm almost 18. I'll be positively ancient if I don't find anyone soon, and no one will want to marry me!"

Grace laid the apple peel on the table in front of her, taking time to make sure she didn't break it. She stood up, turned to her right three times and then to the left three times. As she did so, she repeated a chant of her own creation:

Spirit of the apple tree,

here I twirl for all to see.

Take this peel, o spirit above,

let it tell me of my love."

As she said the word "love," Grace picked up the apple peel between two fingers and threw it over her right shoulder. She stood still, counting silently to five. She turned in place and looked down at the floor where the peel had landed. Everyone in the Wye Valley knew that if you threw an unbroken apple peel over your right shoulder, it might take the shape of the letter of the name of the person you were destined to marry.

"Mrs. Beaton," she called. "Please come and help me. What letter do you think this is?"

Mrs. Beaton took a slow step toward the apple peel and studied it.

"Well," she said, "it's hard to say."

"You always say that," objected Grace.

"Well, dearie," said Mrs. Beaton," "'tis always true. But let's take a better look," she said, as she bent closer to the kitchen floor.

"Do you think it might be an L?" asked Grace. "Or perhaps a P?"

"An L or a P are both possible," replied Mrs. Beaton.

"You always agree with me," Grace protested.

"Perhaps we both see things the same way," said Mrs. Beaton, with a smile. They both stood up. Grace picked up the peel and walked over to put it into the scraps bucket. Then she turned to her friend.

"How am I ever going to find my own true love?" she sighed. "I never go anywhere except to church on Sunday. I never meet anyone new. There is no one suitable for me in the village. All the men are too young or too old. And even if someone came along, unless he was at least an earl, my trustees wouldn't approve of him. I should be having my come out this spring, but the trustees say that there isn't enough money. How am I going to find my true love?"

Mrs. Beaton sighed. Grace was such a good, sweet girl. Was there a way of thwarting the trustees' plans for her marriage?

Grace sat down at the table.

"L might stand for Lionel," she said, "or Leopold. Even Lucifer, although I hope not." How could she ever love a Lucifer? P could stand for Percival or Paul," she continued.

"How will I know?

"There will be a Winter Faire in town soon," said Mrs. Beaton. "People from other villages will be there. Perhaps you will meet someone there."

Grace thought for a minute.

"When we go, I can listen to people speaking to one another," she said. "Perhaps I will hear someone addressed as Lionel or Paul! If so, I will find a way to introduce myself," Grace said with a mischievous smile.

"We'll go together, my lamb," said Mrs. Beaton. "Now that you're almost 18, you shouldn't go out in public without a chaperone. It isn't right for an earl's granddaughter, even if we do live in the country, to go about alone. Surely when you meet your own true love, he will want to know that he's marrying a young woman who was properly raised and chaperoned, one without a stain on her reputation."

Grace smiled. Mrs. Beaton believed that Grace was destined for a ton marriage. Before Grace was born, Mrs. Beaton had worked in London in the home of a duke. She thought that she knew all about the life of the ton.

When the duke had died, his heir had shut down their London home and Mrs. Beaton had returned to her home near Emrall Vale.

Mrs. Beaton's aunt, Emrall Vale's cook, had decided to retire from service and suggested her niece as her replacement. Glad to escape the bad air of the city, Mrs. Beaton had been delighted to settle back into the rural home of a viscount and viscountess.

Grace's father had been a wealthy viscount who had grown up in Emrall Vale. Her mother was the daughter of an earl. They had met at a village fair when her mother was visiting a friend who lived nearby. They married and settled down to start a family.

Grace had been born a year after Mrs. Beaton had come to work in her parents' home.

Mrs. Beaton was worried about Grace and determined to thwart the trustees' plans. She wouldn't let them marry her off to a man who didn't love her. She had a plan.

Every winter, a Romany clan, the Ravenal family, came to the Faire to sell their horses and various tools, kitchenware and woven goods. The matriarch of the clan, Mommia Ravenal, always accompanied them and told fortunes. She and Mrs. Beaton were long-time friends.

Unlike some people who told fortunes, Mommia Ravenal actually had the Sight. Some years ago, Mrs. Beaton had confided her fears for Grace's future. Mommia had promised that, when the time was right, she would do everything she could to help Grace find her own true love.

"If ever the time was right," thought Mrs. Beaton, "that time is now!" She hoped Mommia agreed. Perhaps they could work together to help Grace avoid the fate her trustees had planned for her. The best way would be to find a suitable man that Grace could love. Was there a man anywhere, who was worthy of her?

October.

Every Sunday morning, Grace woke early so that she could break her fast before walking to church with Mrs. Beaton. She hurried through her morning preparations and ran down to the kitchen. There were always muffins for the morning meal on Sundays, along with Mrs. Beaton's delicious mixed-berry compote and butter.

Grace always listened for the early church bells on Sunday morning so that they would know when it was time to leave the house. The wind seemed to carry the chimes all the way from the village to Emrall Vale.

As Grace slipped into her seat at the table, Mrs. Beaton brought her a bowl of porridge topped with a sprinkle of cinnamon and a drizzle of honey from Emrall Vale's own hives. Grace smiled up at Mrs. Beaton in thanks.

"Good morning," she said. "Did you sleep well?"

"As well as a woman my age can sleep," replied Mrs. Beaton. "And you?"

"As well as a woman my age can sleep," responded Grace. They both smiled at their daily joke.

"What do you think Vicar Cauldwell will speak about this morning?" asked Grace.

The topic and length of the vicar's sermon was a subject of much interest in the village. He was an inconsistent speaker. His best sermons were short, to the point and about things related to events in the village. His worst sermons were very long and rambling, based on some esoteric point of ecclesiastic law. As they walked to church, Grace and Mrs. Beaton liked to speculate about which type of sermon they would hear.

Grace enjoyed going into the village to attend services. It was the one time during the week that she interacted with people other than those who lived at Emrall Vale. While everyone in the village was polite to Grace, she had never made any friends. There were no other young women close to her in age. Without parents to introduce her into local society, she was something of a social misfit. No one seemed to know where she belonged in their highly stratified village society.

Walking to church each week, Grace would dream that perhaps, on this particular Sunday, there would be someone new to meet. Someone who might see her, not as the village orphan, but as a young woman worthy of notice. In the last year or so, she had begun to wish that the new person might be a handsome young man who would instantly fall in love with her and marry her. This had never happened, but that fact did not keep Grace from wishing that it might.

On this particular Sunday, as they walked into the village, Mrs. Beaton confided to Grace that the next day they would start making their Christmas cake. Grace smiled. This was one of her favorite activities in the Emrall Vale kitchen. Like all good fruitcake, it took several months to age, so it had to be made well before Christmas.

Mrs. Beaton had a special recipe that had been handed down from mother to daughter for many generations in her family. No one really knew the origin of the recipe. She had once told Grace that her mother believed the recipe had been given to the family by fairies!

Mrs. Beaton always added three shillings to the batter, after which she and Grace mixed it one final time. Miraculously, when they ate the cake during the Christmas season, Grace always got a piece of cake with a shilling in it. She collected these shillings and saved them in an enameled snuff box that had belonged to her father. She never spent them. She called the collection her "Christmas shillings."

It wasn't until the Christmas that Grace was 15, that she realized she had eaten six slices of Christmas cake that year and had gotten six shillings. She knew that Mrs. Beaton only put three shillings in the batter. How had that amount grown to six? With a flash of insight, Grace realized that her friend must have been inserting a shilling into every slice of Christmas Cake that she served Grace. Because of Mrs. Beaton, Grace had a small, but growing nest egg. She was overcome by the love of such a gesture, but she never let on that she had guessed Mrs. Beaton's secret.

Ever since she was a little girl, Grace had loved helping Mrs. Beaton bake the fruitcake. Besides making sure that all the ingredients were correctly prepared, they each made a private wish when they stirred the batter for the final time. In order for the wish to come true, it had to be kept a secret. And Grace knew what she was going to wish for tomorrow. If the letters L and P featured prominently in her wish, who was to know?

A perfect accessory for a quick getaway

CHAPTER FOUR
In which a troubling letter is received.

The next morning, Grace was up and dressed before Mrs. Beaton came to wake her. She was so excited. She wanted to get as much time to bake as possible.

She raced down the stairs, expecting to see Mrs. Beaton preparing bread for the week. Instead, her beloved friend was sitting at the table holding a letter. Tears were sliding down her soft cheeks.

"What's wrong?" cried Grace. "Has someone died?" She swiftly came to her friend's side and threw her arms around the older woman.

Mrs. Beaton put her hand in the pocket of her apron, pulled out a handkerchief and dried her eyes.

"Oh, my dear," she said. "I so hoped and prayed that this news would not come so quickly. Over the last year, with every letter from your trustees, I grew more and more concerned."

"Whatever can it be, to upset you so? Is there no money? Are we to lose our home?" asked Grace.

"No," said Mrs. Beaton. "It's much worse than that. Much, much worse!" And she began to cry again.

"Oh, please don't cry," pleaded Grace. "It can't be so very terrible! Let me see the letter."

With a deep sigh, Mrs. Beaton extended the letter to Grace, who down at the table and began to read.

Dear Mrs. Beaton,

It has come to our attention that Lady Grace will turn 18 on the 31st of December. Now that she is of marriageable age, and there is no one to see to her come out in society, we have taken the step of arranging a suitable match for her.

The 7th Earl of Nottingham has heard of Lady Grace's beauty, intelligence and pretty manners. He applied to us, suggesting a match. Naturally, we were delighted. The Nottingham title is regarded as one of the most prestigious in the ton. The earl himself is a recent, childless widower of 38 and is considered a very desirable match. He is handsome, well respected, and is in possession of all his own hair and teeth. This is a real coup for a young lady without social connections.

The earl has asked that the wedding take place on January 1 at St George's Hanover Square, the parish church of Mayfair, where the earl resides in London. The ceremony will take place at 11 am. Lady Grace is to arrive in London on December 31 with you acting as chaperone. The earl will send a traveling coach with outriders to escort you both to London.

You will both stay with the earl's aunt, the Dowager Countess Tisdale, who will arrange for Lady Grace to appear at the church at the proper time. After the wedding, the couple will immediately begin their wedding trip to the earl's castle in Ireland, where they will reside for several months.

After the wedding, the earl's coach will return you to Emrall Vale. We request that you spend the month of January preparing the

house for the sale of the estate. After January 31, your services will
no longer be needed.

We thank you for your long years of dedicated service to the
Cooper family. Although no provision for a pension for you was
made in the viscount's will, we have deemed it proper to pay your
current wages through January 31 and to give you a gift of 10
pounds in appreciation for your care of Lady Grace.

The earl has asked that we tell you to please see that
Lady Grace is outfitted for her wedding and her new status as the
Countess of Nottingham. The bills for new clothing and accessories
should be sent to us. We are authorized to tell you that you may
spend up to 20 pounds for these items and up to an additional 5
pounds for new shoes.

We wish Lady Grace happy on her auspicious betrothal.
Yrs very truly,
Messers Grimble, Sykes and Cranksley

Grace's face was white and drawn as she finished reading
this letter.

"What can this mean?" she asked Mrs. Beaton. "It sounds like
I will not even get to meet this man until I show up at the church!
How could they do such an awful thing?" She began to cry. "And
you're to leave here with no pension! Where will you go? How will
you manage? What will I do without you?"

"Hush, my sweet," said Mrs. Beaton. "My sister will be happy
to have me as company, now that her children are out of the house.
Her husband is gone. If that doesn't suit, I have enough money
to buy a cottage and support myself. Don't you worry about me.
I'm more concerned about you! I've suspected that they might
attempt something like this for some time, but I didn't think it
would be so soon."

"What are we going to do?" asked Grace.

"We will have to think about this," responded Mrs. Beaton, taking
a deep breath. "We should speak to Mommia. She'll be in the village

for the Winter Faire. In the meantime, there is my special fruitcake to make this morning. You're going to help me, aren't you?"

"Oh yes!" said Grace, drying her eyes. Then tears welled up again. "Especially if this is the last time we will bake fruitcake together." Neither of them saw Juno curled up near the warm kitchen hearth, listening to all that was said.

She was following the conversation between Mrs. Beaton and Grace attentively. *What she heard she didn't like. Marry off her little kit to a man sight unseen? Ridiculous! Even worse, she suspected that the man was the evil-smelling yellow-haired man who had visited when the weather was warmer. It was unthinkable.*

After the baking had been completed, Juno would visit her friends in the stable. They had been lax in their planning to keep their girl safe. Now they must act! But their planning could wait a few hours. Juno enjoyed being in the kitchen when Mrs. Beaton was working. There were always treats on offer and tasty snacks that somehow escaped the tabletop and landed right where Juno happened to be resting.

Mrs. Beaton and Grace worked on the fruitcake most of the morning. Juno made sure to frequently brush against Grace's legs, sending her love and reassurance with each pass.

When all the ingredients had been combined and the batter was ready to be transferred into its baking pans, Mrs. Beaton sent Grace to summon Young Quinn and Miss Prentice. Grace had not had lessons this morning so that she could bake with Mrs. Beaton.

Grace soon came running into the kitchen, a letter in her hand.

"Miss Prentice is gone!" she cried. "She left a note! And Young Quinn is gone with her!" Grace handed the note to Mrs. Beaton.

Mrs. Beaton,

I have been informed by the trustees that my services are to be terminated effective immediately. With the letter they sent me, they enclosed a reference and my wages through last week.

For some time now, Quinn and I have considered ourselves

betrothed and have been planning to move on. We are moving to another part of the country and will be off at first light this morning. We wish you both well.

Yr Humble Servant, Harriett Prentice

Mrs. Beaton stared down at the letter. Her first thought was, "Good riddance to bad rubbish." She had never liked Miss Prentice. However, the loss of Young Quinn was a blow.

Keeping the estate going without Miss Prentice would not be a problem, but without Young Quinn, they would have to sell their horses. Mrs. Beaton and Grace would have a hard time keeping up with the cooking, cleaning and taking care of the animals. In addition, they would be virtually isolated. Although they could walk to the village, going anywhere else would be difficult. She wondered what new disasters lay ahead …

A vardo fit for the matriarch of the clan

CHAPTER FIVE

In which we meet Mommia Ravenal, a seer and healer.

A Romany encampment at Ravens Keep, the estate of Viscount Ravenscrofft in the Wye Valley.

Mommia Ravenal was the matriarch of the formerly itinerant Ravenal Romany clan and kin to the Sinclair family, the Viscounts Ravenscrofft. Her family had recently made the decision to settle on these lands, rather than continue to travel throughout England and the continent. A large section of Ravens Keep had been made over for their use.

Mommia was sitting in front of her vardo, her elegant horsedrawn home that served as the seat of her power within the clan.

One of Mommia's many young male relatives had kindled a small fire for her. She leaned toward it with outstretched hands. It was getting cold.

The clan had convened and decided that those who wished to live at the Keep could do so, and those who wished to live permanently, or occasionally in their vardos, could also do so. Some of the older members found the comfort of the large house, which boasted many fireplaces, a true blessing and a relief for bones that ached in wet or cold weather. However, other older members were still living in their vardos. Usually by October, the clan was on its way to warmer climes. For many of them, this would be their first experience of a winter in England.

It was difficult to give up a home in which one's family had lived for generations. Mommia traveled between both the house, where she slept, and her vardo, where she spent much of her day so that she could be in the heart of her clan. As she sat, wrapped in several layers of soft woolen shawls, she gazed into the fire and thought about the weeks to come.

Everyone was preparing for the Winter Faire. The clan had some excellent young horses to sell, although they would keep the best for themselves or for the Sinclairs. In addition, their clan boasted some of the best weavers in England. They had produced truly magnificent blankets, coats and scarves.

The metalworkers had recently created fireplace sets that had ornate botanical designs on the handles. They were sure to do well as gifts that would appeal to the gentry and the local aristocracy. And, as she had for so many years, Mommia would tell fortunes. She sighed. It was really time to let one of the younger women take over this task. She had been doing it by herself since she was twelve years old. Mommia closed her eyes and remembered.

When she was eight, Mommia had come running to her mother to tell her that one of her younger brothers was in trouble. He had climbed a tree but couldn't get down. He'd been perched in its branches for several hours. After he was rescued, Mommia's mother had questioned Mommia gently. How had she known that her brother was in trouble? What had she felt? Had she seen any pictures in her mind?

The next day, Mommia's mother had requested an audience with her grandmother, the matriarch of their clan. The three women had been seated inside the matriarch's vardo. Mommia's grandmother had taken her Mommia's hands in her own and looked intently at her palms. Then she looked into her granddaughter's eyes.

Even though she was very young, Mommia remembered that look. It seemed to her that her grandmother could see into her most private thoughts and feelings. Mommia loved her grandmother, but she found her a little intimidating. The matriarch was a woman of great majesty and formal bearing. One treated her with the utmost respect.

When Mommia and her mother returned to their vardo, her mother told Mommia that starting the next day, she was to visit her grandmother every afternoon after the midday meal. Mommia was going to learn how to use a very special gift that was the heritage of the women in their family.

Not all the women of the clan had that gift, Mommia's mother explained. Mommia's grandmother was the woman with the greatest manifestation of this particular gift in their clan. It was why she was the matriarch. It was very possible that, since Mommia also had this gift, she would be the matriarch of a clan someday herself. Her grandmother would make sure that she would know how to use the gift wisely and well. The very next day, Mommia began to learn how to use the gift of sight.

Mommia opened her eyes and smiled, remembering those early days. Her grandmother had been an exacting teacher. She had taught Mommia how to sit very quietly for hours at a time, clearing her mind of all thoughts. Sitting still was difficult for an eight-year-old girl, but as she matured, Mommia's ability to still her mind and reach out beyond herself grew, and became as natural as breathing.

At first, it seemed as though everything her grandmother taught her was random. Upon awaking, she must thank the Creator for her life, even before getting out of her bed. She must keep her hands and her person clean at all times. She must be moderate in her eating. She must go outside into a secluded place each day and feel the natural world around her. She must treat all people and all living, growing things as precious gifts brought to life by the Creator.

When Mommia was ten, there was a Faire in a town near their encampment. Grandmother permitted Mommia to come with her to keep her company as she read people's fortunes. Mommia was to sit quietly in the corner and not say a word.

After each person left, Grandmother asked Mommia questions about the person and his or her fortune. Did Mommia think that the fortune was accurate? Did she think the person believed the fortune? Had Mommia's grandmother told the person a true fortune, or just something that would give the person hope?

In this way, Mommia came to understand that fortune telling carried with it great responsibility. She learned that if she saw a bad omen, sometimes she should impart that news, and sometimes she should not. She learned that some people needed to hear a particular fortune even if it was not completely accurate, in order to give them hope for the future.

From that time on, Mommia accompanied her grandmother when she told fortunes. At some point during the day, Grandmother would ask Mommia to do the readings herself. Her grandmother would sit in a padded chair in the corner, seemingly napping. However, Mommia knew that her she was listening. Afterwards, they would discuss the readings and Mommia would ask her grandmother questions.

When she was twelve, her mother and grandmother dressed

her up to look older than she actually was, and took her to a small country fair to do readings by herself. After the day was over, she visited her grandmother in her vardo.

Her grandmother looked very tired. She was lying on her bed covered with beautiful blankets. Mommia knew that her mother had woven them. Her mother was there as well, quiet and somewhat withdrawn.

"My dear one," said her grandmother. "You did well today. We heard people talking about the beautiful new fortuneteller who gave good news and sad news with compassion and love. You have mastered your gift and you will continue to learn and grow.

"Now that you are ready to take my place as the seer of our clan, I can finally go to my reward and join my beloved husband, who awaits me in the beyond."

"No grandmother!" protested Mommia. "Don't leave us! Don't leave me! I still have so much to learn, and I love you so much!"

Mommia's grandmother reached over and took Mommia's soft young hands in her gnarled and spotted ones.

"It is part of the gift that one knows when one's earthly life is coming to a close. I have no fear of death. I have lived a long and useful life and been blessed to train a worthy successor. In time, you will meet a man who is your equal in wisdom and strength, and you will go with him to another clan. That is as it should be.

"In the meantime, you are to inherit this vardo, its contents and all my worldly goods. It contains beloved items that have been passed down from mother to daughter and granddaughter for many generations.

"Some clans have the tradition of burning all of a person's belongings when he or she dies. Our clan does not follow that custom. This vardo and its contents will be your dowry. Hopefully, some of the items will remind you of me when I am long gone. Tell my stories to your children and your grandchildren, for you will be so blessed. Remember that you are beloved and loving."

Mommia's mother was quietly weeping in the corner. Tears were trickling down Mommia's face.

"Grandmother," she said softly, "You have been all that I might have wished for in a teacher. I vow that I will use everything you have taught me for good. I will pass your teachings on to future generations with love in my heart. Please watch over me from the beyond and help me to live a good and righteous life."

Her grandmother gently squeezed Mommia's hands and then looked over to her daughter.

"Come," she said to her. "Sit next to me as I take my last breaths. Sing me that song that I sang to you as a baby."

Mommia and her mother sat on the bed holding the old woman's hands. They sang the lullaby that had been handed down from generation to generation in their family. The rest of the clan, hearing the song, gathered around the vardo and joined their voices to the hymn of farewell.

When the sun dipped below the horizon, the matriarch took a last, deep breath and smiled. She was with her beloved. The singing stopped. The clan knew that their matriarch was gone. One of the horses whinnied, and Mommia was brought back to the present. She realized that tears were streaming down her cheeks. As she brushed them away, she stood up and stretched.

Forcing herself back to the present, Mommia considered the discussion she had with Mrs. Beaton. Her friend had presented her with two problems.

The Emrall Vale's stable master had run off with Grace's governess. Mrs. Beaton had asked Mommia if there might be someone among her kin who would be willing to take charge of their stable and do light repairs around the estate. Mommia had an idea about which of her many nephews might serve well in that capacity.

The other problem was more difficult. As the cards had foretold many years ago, Grace's trustees were plotting to rob her by marrying her off to a wicked, older man. Grace needed a husband to protect her, and quickly. Could the person who went to the estate to be the stable master also be a possible husband for Grace?

Mommia gazed into the fire and then pulled out her personal Tarot deck. She asked her questions, laid out the cards and then sat quietly, gazing at them. After some time, the answer came. Mommia was surprised and pleased. Two birds with one stone …

Hal — a long time ago

CHAPTER SIX

In which we meet our hero,
Hal, or whatever his name is!

Ravens Keep Stables. Later that day.

Lord Harold "Hal" Neil Picton, 10th earl of Langafel, was
hiding from Mommia in the Ravens Keep stables. He had been
having a perfectly fine day, helping his Ravenal cousins train
a new stallion colt. Horses were easy. People were difficult, he
thought. One of his cousins had alerted him that Mommia was
looking for him. Like everyone in the clan, he had learned early on
that when Mommia came looking for you, your life was about to
change. Hal was very happy living with the clan, hiding from his
aristocratic future. He realized, with a sense of resignation that the
time was near when he would have to shoulder the responsibilities
that destiny had laid on his shoulders.

He had been hidden for as long as he could remember. When

his father, the ninth earl, had been a young man just down from Oxford, he had fallen in love with a beautiful Romany woman. He had swept her away from her clan. They married her over the anvil in Gretna Green before either family became aware of the couple's intentions. The newlyweds settled near Edinburgh, while both sets of relatives took time to become reconciled to their marriage. It was a true love match.

Delia Ravenal and August Picton lived happily, if simply, in a small cottage. He taught in the village school. Delia told fortunes. When she became pregnant, the couple were delighted, but their happiness was not to last. Delia's labor was difficult and protracted. Although her son was born alive and healthy, she died just a day after giving birth. Before she died, she asked that her son be named Harold Neil after her father and her uncle. August agreed and the boy was named Harold Neil Picton.

August immediately hired a wet nurse for his son. The woman and her husband lived nearby and had just lost an infant. They offered to foster August's tiny son until long-term plans to care for him could be made. Beside himself with grief, August agreed. Just two days later, he contracted a fever and quickly declined. When he died, the neighbors agreed that the death of his beloved wife had robbed him of the will to live.

When August and Delia's fathers finally tracked down their children, they were devastated to learn that both had died and been buried in the local church yard. Their neighbors, knowing that, for some reason, the young couple were in hiding from their families, did not tell the bereaved fathers that they shared a grandson.

The fathers made significant donations to the church for the upkeep of the graves. Then they turned around and went back to their homes.

It was in this way that Harold Neil Picton, called Hal by all who knew him, came to be raised by Alice and Charles Porter. They were good parents to him and ultimately gave him a beloved younger brother and the sweetest sister in the world.

On his 18th birthday, Alice and Charles took Hal to the graves of his parents and told him the true story, as best they knew it, of his birth. He was shocked, but not especially surprised. At a young age, he realized that he looked different from his parents and his siblings.

Hal was tall, with an athletic build. His skin had a slightly golden tone that was in sharp contrast to Alice and Charles' porcelain coloring. Their eyes – and those of his brother and sister — were blue. His were dark black. Everyone in his family had blond hair. His hair was blue-black. He had a dramatic white shock of hair going from his right temple to the base of his skull.

Alice and Charles explained that they had always loved him as though he was their own son. After all, he had come to them when he was just a day old. They said that they would always consider themselves his parents, and that they hoped he would continue to love his brother and sister. However, they said, it was likely that Delia and August, the parents who had given him birth, had relatives who would welcome him with joy, if they could be found. Would he like to consider trying to find them?

Charles revealed that when Hal's father died, he and Alice had carefully packed away all the couple's belongings. They had kept those few things safe for the day when Hal would be told about his true parentage. There were some items that might hold clues about both families. They suggested that Hal spend some time at the graveside. Perhaps the spirit of those parents would speak to him and guide him. Whatever he decided, they, Alice and Charles, would help him in every way they could.

In the end, Hal set out to find his mother's family, simply because he had a lead on where the family might be. There had been a letter from Delia Ravenal's mother to her daughter with information about the clan's projected travel.

It took Hal two years, traveling from one Romany encampment

to another, to discover that the Ravenal clan had settled on the estate of Viscount Ravenscrofft. By the time he found the clan, his grandmother had died, but one of her younger brothers, Alexandru Ravenal, was still alive and was, in fact, the patriarch of the clan. He was married to Mommia, the clan's seer.

Hal had initially been met with suspicion and hostility. No one had ever heard of him. Delia's disappearance to marry a young lord, however, was part of the clan's lore. Hal told his story to a stony-faced group of elders.

He was asked if he had any proof of his relationship to their beloved Delia. At that point, Hal produced a monogrammed handkerchief that had belonged to his mother.

One of the older women gasped in recognition of the needlework and began to cry. Through her tears, she told Hal that she herself had taught Delia how to make those stitches. She turned the handkerchief over and showed him a small, embroidered letter B. "I put that there myself," she said. "It's for my name, "Bella."

Pandemonium ensued. The women cried. The men alternately slapped Hal on the back and pulled him into crushing hugs. All the while, Mommia Ravenal sat quietly. When things began to settle down, she stood. Silence reigned.

"It is good," she began, "that Hal could show us the handkerchief. He has brought our Delia back so that we can say goodbye to her in a proper manner. But none of you should have needed such proof. He carries the proof of his heritage in his hair."

Mommia walked over to the boy and pulled off his cap. There was a gasp! All eyes were riveted to the white streak of hair running through Hal's thick black locks.

"He bears the sign of the gift of the horse! Only a few members of our clan have that gift. It is unique to the Ravenal family! That streak of white is undeniable proof that he is the son of our lost Delia! One who was lost to us has come home!"

There was more cheering, and crying, feasting, and drinking well into the night. Delia Ravenal's son had been reunited with his clan.

Mommia knew that Hal would eventually get tired of hiding from her and would present himself at her vardo. She just had to wait. He was a good lad, and she was proud of him. When he eventually came to her in the late afternoon, she gestured for him to sit and share a cup of tea with her. Hal smiled when he saw that she was using a very elegant china tea set.

"Do you like this?" she asked him. "It was a gift from Viscount Ravenscrofft when we decided to settle here. He has always been such a generous man."

"It's beautiful," replied Hal, lifting the delicate cup in gentle fingers.

"When you take up your title," said Mommia, "you will have many such things to share with your bride."

"Stallions and mares and all the ships at sea!" thought Hal, "The issue of my title and a bride! My days of hiding are gone."

Hal sighed, and then listened as Mommia described his responsibilities and his future.

Mommia's Striped Tent

CHAPTER SEVEN
In which Lady Grace begins to learn about her future.

A few weeks later.

The day of the Winter Faire dawned crisp and clear. Grace woke up full of energy and anticipation. Mrs. Beaton had told her that they would begin their day at the Faire by going to Mommia to have their fortunes told.

Grace had never done this before, although she had begged Mrs. Beaton every year to take her to the fortune teller's tent. Every year, Mrs. Beaton would say, "It's not yet time." Grace didn't really understand what she meant by this, but the fact that they were going to do it, meant that it was "time." She was very excited.

After a breakfast of porridge and muffins, Grace helped wash the dishes and then went to her bedroom to get her hat and her warmest coat. It was too cold for their old pony to leave the warm stable, so they walked to the Faire.

Along the way, they met neighbors headed in the same direction. Some of them, who were riding in carriages or carts, offered them transportation, but they refused, with thanks. They were enjoying the exercise and the slower pace, which allowed them to listen to birdsong and the rustling of tree branches moving in the wind.

It was ten o'clock in the morning by the time they entered the village square. Grace smiled in appreciation. She always enjoyed her first view of the village. Mrs. Beaton took her hand, and they began to walk toward Mommia's tent.

The tent was made of red and green-striped material and looked very gay. It was set in a quiet corner near the entrance to the surrounding woodland. Long colorful ribbons were attached to all four supporting poles. The ribbons danced in the wind, welcoming all who were curious about their fate. A flag, emblazoned with the Ravenal clan symbol, a raven in flight, fluttered gently in the soft breeze next to the opening of the tent.

Despite the early hour, there were three young women waiting to have their fortunes told. Grace and Mrs. Beaton joined the queue, chatting about their plans for the day.
One of the older children of the family who owned the village tavern, The Hungry Dragon, came by with mugs of hot, spiced cider. Grace and Mrs. Beaton purchased two, and sipped them as they waited.

Grace was unaware of the passage of time. She hadn't forgotten her plan to seek out men whose names started with the letters L and P. She was enjoying being away from the estate with nothing to do but have fun.

When they got to the front of the line, Mrs. Beaton said, "I would like to go in first and greet my friend Mommia." Grace smiled and nodded, absorbed in thinking about all the men's names that could begin with P and L.

It seemed like hardly any time at all when Mrs. Beaton came out of the tent and said, "It's your turn now, Grace. Mommia is looking forward to telling your fortune." Grace entered the tent.

In later years, when Grace thought about her fortune telling session with Mommia at the Winter Faire, what she remembered most was the feeling of being safe and protected in the tent. The setting was nothing like what Grace had expected. There was no crystal ball. There were no cards. There was no reading of tea leaves. Mommia extended her hands toward Grace, and Grace presented her hands to the seer, palms up.

Mommia gazed at Grace's palms intently. After some minutes of silence, she gentle squeezed Grace's hands and returned them to her. Then she smiled.

"There are forces at work in your life which can bring you sorrow, but can also bring you joy," Mommia began. "I know that you wish to marry for love, as so many young women do. For you, it is more important that you marry as soon as possible. You must marry before the New Year."

"So soon?" gasped Grace. "I haven't met my beloved yet. I believe his name begins with an L or a P. I had hoped that I would meet him here at the Faire. How can I marry someone by the New Year when I haven't even met him yet? In such a short time, how will I know if he is truly my intended beloved?"

"You will know that he is your love as soon as you meet him," said Mommia, "even though it may take you a little while to realize that your love, and his, are true and lasting. You must have faith that Mrs. Beaton and I have your welfare as our highest priority. You will question, but ultimately, you must believe in our love for you, for love it truly is."

"Will I meet him today?" asked Grace.

"Yes, you will," said Mommia.

"What is his name?"

"That I cannot tell you," said Mommia.

"But can you tell me if it has an L or P?" Grace persisted. Mommia smiled mysteriously. "I assure you that it does, although it may not seem to be so when you first make his acquaintance. Eventually, the truth will be revealed."

"Is it really necessary to be so mysterious?" Grace asked.

"Of course it is!" Mommia said, amused. "How will you know that he is your true love if you don't find it out for yourself?"

"Mommia," said Grace, "will there be a sign that I can look for, a sign that will tell me if the man I meet is my own true love?

Mommia suddenly looked grave. "It is possible that there will be a sign, but you must uncover it yourself."

"Can't you give me a clue?" pleaded Grace. Mommia sat quietly, as though considering this question. Grace waited. Finally, Mommia said, "Other than Mrs. Beaton, is there anyone else who you would trust with your life and wellbeing?"

Grace thought about that question for a few minutes. Mommia had not said "persons." She had said "anyone else." There were, in fact, several.

"There is Juno, our cat, of course," responded Grace. "You have met her in the woods when she has come to call me home. I have always believed that Juno understands every word I say.

"We also have three horses," she continued. "There is my father's stallion, Blackie, a big black racehorse who no longer likes being ridden. There is my mother's mare, Bronwyn, a bay Arabian who permits me to ride her once in a while. And there is my pony, Boy, who is very old."

"I'm sure that Juno earns her keep policing the mice on the estate," Mommia said. "Three horses, who do no work, however, are expensive to feed and stable. Why have you not sold them? I understand that your trustees keep you on very short funds."

"Oh!" said Grace, "I would never do that! All of the animals on the estate are members of my family! Except for Juno, none of them can do much work anymore. I'm responsible for them. I want to make their old age as comfortable as possible. I go to the stable very day to give them each an apple. Since our stable master left, I clean out their stalls every day and feed and water them as well. And of course, I talk to them."

"What do you talk to them about?" asked Mommia.

"I tell them all my secrets," responded Grace. "When I am sad and missing my parents, I pretend that Blackie is my father, that Bronwyn is my mother, and that Boy is the little child my mother was carrying when she and my father died.

"I talk to them. I tell Blackie things I would like to tell my father. I ask Bronwyn the questions I wish I could ask my mother now that I'm a young woman. And I talk to Boy as though he was my little brother. I tell him how much I love and cherish him."

"Do they talk to you?" asked Mommia.

"I think they do," said Grace. "Sometimes, after I have talked to them, I feel as though I can hear my mother's voice, my father's voice, even my baby brother's voice speaking to me. It makes me feel less lonely. And, of course, I always talk to Juno."

"That is a very good way to treat beings that are special to you. I am sure that they appreciate your love and kindness," said Mommia.

"All animals like to be talked to, even if their language is not like human speech. And because you have such wisdom, I will share a secret with you about your animal friends."

"A secret?" asked Grace.

"Yes. This is a secret known only to my clan. We have 'the gift of the horse'." Some of the members of the clan understand the language of horses. It is a very special talent. The members of our clan who have it are born with a streak of white hair that goes from their right temple to the back of their skull. Because of this special ability, we also know that once a year, on the midnight that falls between Christmas Eve and Christmas Morning, some people who do not have the gift of the horse, can understand the speech of animals!"

"Do you mean," asked Grace breathlessly, "that if I were to go into our barn on that midnight, I could understand what the horses were saying?"

"Only people who are loved by the horses can be so blessed. From what you have told me, I am sure that your horses love you very much. But you cannot just go into the stable and wait to hear them speak. There are certain customs that must be observed."

"What customs?" asked Grace, intrigued.

"I will tell you," said Mommia, "but my old bones are getting stiff. I need to take a walk in the woods to loosen up and refresh myself. I can tell that you also need some time to think. My young apprentice can tell fortunes for a while."

Mommia turned to the back of the tent where a young woman of perhaps 14 or 15 was sitting quietly. Grace hadn't noticed her before.

"Come Sibella," Mommia said softly. "Take my place until I return."

The tall, reed-thin young woman stood and walked over to where Mommia had been sitting. Grace noticed that she had clear green eyes and a golden complexion. Her black hair was pulled back into a knot at the back of her head, and her hair was covered with a brightly colored scarf.

"Thank you, Mommia," Sibella said, her voice light and clear.

"I will keep in mind all that you have taught me and be gentle and loving to all who enter this tent."

"I could ask for no more," replied Mommia, smiling. "You will do well."

Turning to Grace she said, "Come and walk with me silently in the woods. When our spirits feel rested, we will return and continue our discussion.

"Yes, of course, Mommia," said Grace. "Whatever you wish."

Mommia wrapped herself in a heather-blue woolen cape.

"Come," she said. "It's just the right time to hear the birds sing love songs to one another. Remember, we must remain quiet. "

She took Grace's hand. They left the tent together, walking toward the winter woods.

Enchantment in the forest

CHAPTER EIGHT
*In which Hal's bride
is revealed to him.*

Hal took a deep breath. He loved being alone in the woods. Alone, that is, except for all the trees and the animals. He had taken a break from helping with the horses at the Faire. His Ravenal cousins could handle things without him for a while. After his conversation with Mommia, Hal realized that, at 26, after six years in hiding with the clan, it was time for him assume the responsibilities that came with his father's heritage and find a wife. He had already begun to process of learning about the earldom.

Six months before the Faire, Hal had received a packet from his foster mother with some of his favorite shortbread, a note and an unopened letter that looked very important. It was written on thick paper and had the name of a firm of solicitors as the return address.

His foster mother explained in her note, that the enclosed letter had come to the church with a request for information about any children of the late August Picton, who was buried in the church yard. The vicar, aware of the circumstances of Hal's birth, had passed the letter along to his foster parents. They were now forwarding the letter to him.

The contents of the letter were a surprise. The solicitors identified themselves as representatives of the 8th Earl of Langafel, recently deceased. The earl's heir, August Picton, the 9th earl, had died many years ago. The solicitors were now looking for any living male relatives to avoid the extinction of the title. They asked that anyone with knowledge come to London to meet with them as soon as possible.

Hal had stared at the letter, horrified. He was an earl? The 10th Earl of Langafel? How could this be? What would happen if he didn't reply? Would the solicitors come looking for him? Did he want to be found?

He had discussed the situation with Mommia and Alexandru. They urged him to take time to make up his mind. Once he stepped into the role of earl, he could never truly return to the life of the Rom. They assured him, however, that he would always be a member of their clan and a welcome visitor.

Hal considered their advice. He had taken a few weeks to think about what he should do. At Alexandru's urging, Hal had requested a meeting with Viscount Ravenscrofft, the master of Ravens Keep. The Viscount had explained both the joys and the serious responsibilities of inheriting a title. After that meeting, Hal realized that he could not, in good conscience, do anything but write to the solicitors and let them know that they had found the 10th Earl of Langafel.

Needless to say, the solicitors had been overjoyed to hear that there was a direct heir to the title. Since then, Hal had been to London several times to meet with them and he had begun to take up the reigns of the earldom. Hal's solicitors had reviewed his financial status with him. Apparently, his ancestors had been very shrewd about managing their assets. The earldom's coffers were overflowing.

The family seat, near Farnham in Surrey, the solicitors assured Hal, was being well managed by the estate's long-time steward. On one of his trips to London, Hal met the family's man of business and his son. The older man was planning to retire. His son, who had been working for him for several years, would be taking over his father's role as the earldom's man of business. The three men agreed that they would meet at the earldom's seat near Farnham after the New Year to create a plan for helping Hal settle into his new life.

As Hal walked through the woods, he found himself thinking about how his life would change once he truly assumed full responsibility for the earldom. The woods were quiet. He stopped under a massive oak tree and leaned against its comforting trunk. Hal felt agitated and somewhat adrift. The solidity of the tree felt reassuring.

"The woods are so still," he thought, and then changed his mind. Not far from where he stood, he saw two women walking together. Even at a distance, he recognized Mommia. Her companion was a young woman he had seen before, but had never met.

Hidden in the darkness of the towering trees, he observed them. He saw a bright shaft of light break through the tops of the trees. It shone down on the young woman, completely enveloping her. It was as though she was aglow. She looked like an angel.

The young woman looked up into the brightness. As he watched, entranced, she threw back her head and laughed, raising her hands toward the sun.

Hal had never seen a sight like that in his life. Unbidden, a picture came into his mind. He and the young woman were standing side by side on a hilltop, looking down on a valley carpeted with bluebells. With a shock of recognition, Hal realized that bluebells symbolize everlasting love. In his vision, he saw several children with sparkling eyes and shining blue-black hair. They were laughing and running through the valley.

The picture was so vivid, Hal reached out to gently stroke the woman's face, only to find nothing but air. The trance was broken by a raven's cry. This area of the Wye Valley was home to many distinctive flocks of ravens. He blinked. The two women had moved on, walking back in the direction of the village.

Hal stood still, thinking about what had just happened. He had lived with the Ravenal Clan long enough to recognize a sign when it occurred. Especially when it was announced by a raven. Thinking back to his talk with Mommia, he realized that the young woman he had just seen must be his intended bride. It could not be coincidental that Hal had seen the young woman just as he was wondering about whether or not to accept his title. Should he choose to accept the life of an earl, having a countess would be an enormous help. How wonderful it would be to have a wife whose laugh could be coaxed into being by sunshine.

Hal had not had much intimate experience with women. Actually, not any, except for once being kissed by a friend's older sister behind the church. Shortly after he had settled in with his Ravenal relatives, Alexandru had taken Hal for a long walk and explained the rules by which the Rom conducted relationships between men and women. Discovering that Hal knew nothing of adult romance, Alexandru spent quite some time educating his young charge about proper intimate relations between people who loved one another.

When they returned to camp, Alexandru went into his vardo and came out with a large, leather-bound book secured by a heavy, bronze clasp. He presented it to Hal. The book had pictures of men and women in various intimate positions.

"A gift," Alexandru had said, "to help build a happy marriage."

Hal had never seen such a book before. Some of the pictures were very intriguing, while others looked, frankly, impossible.

Now, probably very soon, based on what Mommia had said about her young friend's situation, Hal was going to have the opportunity to experience a new part of adult life. Having a wife might be a very interesting adventure …

A precious heirloom

CHAPTER NINE
In which Lady Grace learns how to talk to her animal friends.

When Mommia and Grace returned to Mommia's tent, they both felt refreshed. Grace had been startled by the shaft of light that had broken through the canopy of the trees. She felt as though she was being hugged in a loving embrace by the sun. She had laughed with joy. The birds, the trees, even the wind were all whispering to her, sharing their secrets. And Grace was listening.

Grace and Mommia resumed their seats in the tent. The older woman addressed her.

"Let's get back to our discussion. How do you think you can convince your animals to speak with you at midnight on Christmas Eve?" asked Mommia.

Grace sat silently for a minute, thinking about what her animals might like. After a short silence, she replied, "I have no idea. I never knew that they could talk."

"Animals love to talk to their people," said Mommia. "Most people don't know that secret. It's all a matter of strategy. You can't just expect them to speak. You have to let them know that you are ready to listen to them."

"How do I do that?" asked Grace, excitement mounting.

"It will take time, preparation and love," replied Mommia. "There is a ritual you must perform. You will begin eight days before Christmas Eve."

"Why eight days?" Grace asked, puzzled.

"Eight is a special number in many cultures," responded Mommia. "When you draw an eight, you are creating the sign of something that has no beginning and no end. There is an ancient teaching that eight is a number associated with new beginnings."

Grace traced the number eight on the tabletop and looked at it thoughtfully.

"I never thought of numbers having secret meanings," she said.

"The world is much greater than that which we can perceive through our five senses," responded Mommia. "Our lives gain in richness and variety when we open ourselves to all that exists."

"I love that idea," said Grace. "I'm so excited that Blackie, Bronwyn and Boy, and even Juno, might wish to speak to me. But how do I let them know I'm listening?"

Mommia reached across the table and took Grace's hand, holding it firmly and looking into the girl's eyes.

"Here is what you must do," the older woman said. "Nine days before Christmas Eve, buy a variety of colored ribbons. The next day, bring them with you when you visit your animals. Show each ribbon to each one. Notice their reactions. Which colors seem to attract them and which colors do not interest them.

"Talk to each animal. Ask each one which color it likes best. Do this every day, eliminating the colors they don't seem to like until you know which color is most desired by which animal.

"Why do you say 'animals' rather than 'horses?'" asked Grace.

"We only have horses in the barn."

"You should include Juno in this activity," said Mommia. "You may also find that there will be other types of animals in your barn as Christmas Eve approaches."

"How very odd," thought Grace.

Mommia continued with her instructions.

"During the day leading up to Christmas Eve, you must curry all the horses and any other large animals. Brush Juno's fur, if she will permit it. Wipe them all down with warm, damp cloths and braid their manes with ribbons of the correct color. If she will allow it, tie the ribbon of Juno's choice loosely around her neck. If she doesn't seem to like that, tie it to her bed.

"On the day of Christmas Eve," said Mommia, "you must feed each horse or other animal his or her favorite food. I assume you know what that is?"

"Oh yes!" said Grace. "We can't always give them those foods, but I certainly know what they each prefer."

"Talk to Mrs. Beaton. Tell her what we've discussed. She will see to it that those foods are available for you."

"I will," said Grace. "I have no secrets from Mrs. Beaton. She has always taken care of me and shown me nothing but love."

"You are fortunate in having her to care for you." said Mommia. "She is pure of heart."

Grace nodded.

"Now," said Mommia, "let us go back to your Christmas Eve preparations. The next step is very important.

"An hour before midnight, you must come to the stable and ask your animals for forgiveness. Did you forget one day to give them their apples? Were you lazy about cleaning out their stalls? Did you let their water get musty?

"You must confess all your wrong doing, separately to each animal. You must promise to do better in the coming year. You must ask each one humbly for his or her forgiveness."

"How will I know that they have forgiven me?" asked Grace, worried.

"When the bell in the church strikes twelve," replied Mommia, "if they have forgiven you, they will allow you to understand their language. If they do so, you may ask them any questions you wish."

"That would be so wonderful," replied Grace. "How will I know what to ask?"

Mommia nodded.

"I've never known you to be at a loss for words."

Grace smiled shyly.

"Talk to them about whatever you wish," Mommia said. "If they desire to do so; they will speak to you. All equines are very wise. You will have all night to speak with them; all night until the first ray of dawn breaks over the horizon. At that point, you will no longer be able to understand their speech."

"Are they seers?" asked Grace. "Will they be able to tell me who my own true love is? When I will meet him?"

"Horses are not seers," answered Mommia, "but they notice things that humans sometimes do not see."

"What kind of things?" asked Grace.

"People often communicate without words," said Mommia. "They reveal their true nature and feelings by their actions. Horses understand these silent messages."

"I always wondered what Blackie was thinking he saw Young Quinn speaking to my governess," said Grace. "He seemed to be suspicious of them. Ever since they went away, I've wondered if he knew something I didn't."

"That's very possible," said Mommia.

"Is there anything else I need to know about talking to our animals?" Grace asked.

Mommia pressed her lips together, taking a deep breath. She was silent for several moments. Grace wondered if she would answer her question. Finally, Mommia spoke.

"I will tell you a very special secret, known only to members of our clan. Horses like to play tricks on humans! They think it's great fun.

"When the horses talk to you, they won't lie, but they may answer you indirectly. If you wish to know the identity of your true love, the may answer you with a riddle you will have to solve."

"I've never had to solve a riddle before," said Grace. "What if I can't figure it out?

"The horses have a different sense of humor than that of humans," replied Mommia. It may take a while, but in the end, all will be revealed."

Mommia sat back and was silent. Grace sat silently too. After a few minutes, she asked, "Is that all?"

"Yes, my dear," said Mommia. "That is all for today. After the Faire, if you have other questions, come to my vardo in the Ravenscrofft forest and I will welcome you."

"Thank you, Mommia," said Grace, getting to her feet. "Mrs. Beaton said that when you tell people's fortunes, they are supposed to give you something of value in return. I don't have any coin. The thing I value most in the world is a silver locket that belonged to my mother."

Grace took the silver locket from around her neck and handed it to Mommia.

"Thank you for helping me, Mommia. I appreciate what you have told me. I will follow all your instructions."

Mommia reached forward and let Grace place the locket in her outstretched hand.

"I have never before received a gift of such value," she said, her eyes grave. "I pledge that one day you will be reunited with it. When you are, you will know that you have found your own true love."

Grace gasped and tears came to her eyes. She moved toward

the woman and threw her arms around her. "Thank you," she said. "Thank you!"

"Go now," said Mommia. "Mrs. Beaton wants to show you our beautiful horses."

Grace left the tent and found Mrs. Beaton waiting for her.

"Well? Did Mommia give you a good fortune?" she asked.

"I'm not sure it was a fortune," said Grace, "but now I know how I might be able to find my own true love."

Mrs. Beaton smiled. "That's good then," she said. "Come, let's go see the horses. Mommia said that there are several that are quite special."

The older woman and her charge began to walk toward the opposite end of the village where the horses were on display. Grace barely noticed the bustling people around her, so intently was she trying to understand all the things that Mommia had told her.

It was with surprise that her nose told her they had reached the field in which the horses were kept. Grace came to herself and began to look at each of the beautiful animals that Mommia's kin had brought to the Faire.

"What do you think of that bay horse with the matching white stockings?" asked Mrs. Beaton, pointing to one of the horses on the far side of the enclosure. Grace looked at the animal intently.

"He's very flashy," she said. "I think that he would do well for a young man who lives in London and would like to ride him in a park. I have the feeling that horse doesn't like to work too hard."

Mrs. Beaton laughed. "Which one would you choose if you could have any horse in the paddock?" she asked. This was a game they played every year. They both knew that there was no money to buy Grace her own mount. However, they enjoyed playing the game nevertheless.

Grace looked carefully at every horse. Each one was beautiful and had something to recommend it. In the farthest corner, a particular animal caught her eye.

"Do you see that little grey donkey in the corner?" she asked Mrs. Beaton. "That is the animal I would bring home with me if I could."

"The little donkey?" Mrs. Beaton asked, surprised. "I can hardly see you hacking down the country lanes on that poor beast! Why, it doesn't look like it has long for this world! Why would you choose the donkey?"

"I think it's sad and lonely," said Grace. "I don't think there's anything wrong with it. I just think it's given up hope. If I could take him home, I would visit him every day, tell him all my secrets and ask him to take me to church each Sunday."

Mrs. Beaton laughed. The sound attracted the notice of the most handsome man Grace had ever seen. He had been currying a tall, white stallion with a mane braided with a red ribbon. The stallion had the slightly concave nose that marked him as an Arabian steed. The man stopped his labor and walked over to Grace and Mrs. Beaton.

Grace's heart began to beat wildly in her breast. Her knees felt weak and she grabbed the fence of the pen to keep from falling to the ground. "Holy apple peels! I hope his name starts with a P or an L!"

Balthazar – a very special donkey

CHAPTER TEN
In which Balthazar finds a new home.

The man was taller than all the men around him. He had a slight, golden cast to his skin. His nose looked like it had been broken at least once. He had the deepest, darkest black eyes Grace had ever seen. His lips were lush and supple. Grace wondered what it would be like to nibble on them. She barely noticed the horse-shaped gold stud glinting in his left earlobe.

The most remarkable thing about this man was his hair. Grace gasped. Glistening blue-black locks were pulled into a queue with a red leather tie. From the man's right temple all the way to the back of his head was a thick streak of silver-white hair. This man, who carried himself like a prince, had the gift of the horse! Grace couldn't take her eyes off him. She wondered if she had ever seen him before. She didn't think so, yet there was something familiar about him.

He walked over to them, bowed, and addressed Mrs. Beaton.

"I heard you laugh. That laugh is the loveliest sound I have heard all day," he said. "Do I have the honor of meeting the famous Mrs. Beaton and her lovely charge, Lady Grace Cooper? Mommia, my aunt, said that you might stop by."

Hal realized that the young woman standing in front of him was the vision he had seen in the forest.

"Here she is," he thought. "My future bride."

Mrs. Beaton beamed at him.

"Harold Neil," he continued, pausing before saying his last name. "Ravenal. Harold Neil Ravenal."

"So nice to meet you, Mr. Ravenal," said Mrs. Beaton. "Mommia has spoken of you."

"Please call me Hal," he said. "Mr. Ravenal' makes me feel like a great uncle who has been deceased for twenty years!"

"If you feel like a man who's been deceased for twenty years," said Grace without thinking, "you must feel very poorly indeed!"

Then a look of surprise and consternation washed over her face. Her hand flew up to cover her mouth. Had she just said such an impertinent thing to a strange man? What was wrong with her?

Hal threw back his head and laughed for what seemed, to Grace, to be forever! It was a sweet sound that she wished would never end.

Mrs. Beaton turned to her in surprise. "Grace!" she exclaimed. The man, Hal, pulled himself together and looked at Grace with amusement.

"I must say, Lady Grace, you have made my day! It's refreshing to meet a young lady with such a quick wit."

"And," Hal thought to himself, "you are so very, very lovely."

She was to be his future countess. Meeting her made him absolutely positive that she was the one woman for him. Suddenly, colors were brighter, the mixed smells of horses and food and fresh hay were stronger and sweeter. The day suddenly seemed warmer.

Grace stood before him, her eyes lowered and a tiny smile on her raspberry-red lips. She was adorable!

"Get yourself together, man." Hal remonstrated with himself. "You're going to pieces!" He had a mission to accomplish. For a moment, he wondered what the mission was. Then he remembered.

"Mommia said that you might be in the market for an addition to your stable. Is there one here that meets with your approval?" he asked.

"Oh no!" said Grace, "we can't afford, I mean we have no need, I mean…" Grace stopped, not knowing what to say. Why would Mommia have told this god-like creature that she was looking for a new animal friend?

"Come, come," said Hal gently. "If you could have any one of these truly remarkable creatures…" he extended his well-muscled arm to indicate all the inhabitants of the paddock, "which one would you choose?"

"How does he know that Mrs. Beaton and I play that game every time we come to the Faire?" thought Grace.

"How about that flashy bay with the white stockings?" Hal asked.

"Oh no!" said Grace without thinking. "He's not for the country, although I think he'd like the city well enough."

Hal smiled approvingly at Grace. "Quite right, and quite astute, my lady," he said. "Young Strider there is a fribble and would do well as a mount for a fribble of the ton!"

Grace laughed at the joke.

"What about my Arabian friend here," Hal continued. "Surely, he finds favor in your sight."

Grace sighed. "He's lovely, but too fine for me to ride on humble country lanes. He deserves to be in the company of other horses like himself."

"Nothing is too fine for you, Lady Grace," she thought she heard the man whisper, but she couldn't believe he would say such a thing. It was almost as if she heard his voice in her mind.

"Ah well," she heard Hal say in his normal, rich baritone. "Is there any poor creature here that, given the opportunity, you would wish to bring home?"

"I wish I could bring that poor little donkey in the corner home with me," said Grace. "He seems lost among all these noble creatures."

"Tell me about the animals in your stable," asked Hal, seeming to change the subject.

Grace told him about Blackie, Bronwyn and Boy.

"Do you have them in work?" Hal asked.

"Oh no!" replied Grace. "They're all too old to do very much. On a Sunday, if Boy isn't feeling achy, he will pull the pony cart so that Mrs. Beaton and I can ride to church. Most of the time they are all out in the pasture, and of course they come into the stable at night."

"Surely your stable master could find something more productive for them to do?" Hal suggested.

Grace looked down, feeling sad.

"We no longer have a stable master," she replied. "He recently ran off with my governess. We haven't replaced him," she said, and then her voice trailed off.

"Who takes care of the horses then?" Hall asked.

Mrs. Beaton took up the chore of explaining their household arrangements.

"Right now, Lady Grace has taken on the work of seeing to the horses. Once a week, a young assistant groom who works on the next estate comes in to do the heavy work. For right now, we are managing. Going forward, we will have to see."

Hal listened to this sad tale without any expression crossing his face. Why wasn't anyone taking better care of this lovely young woman? Mommia had told him that the family had plenty of money. Why wasn't it being used for Grace's benefit? Hal was touched by the way Grace cared for her horses and didn't complain about her circumstances. As Mommia had told him, she was a very unusual young woman.

"Wouldn't having the donkey in the stable add to your work, since you have no stable master?" Hal asked.

"Oh no!" said Grace. "I think the horses would enjoy having a new companion. And he's so little. He wouldn't be a burden at all!"

"You shall have him, then!" said Hal decisively.

"But I couldn't," said Grace. "I don't have any money, any real money that is. Even though he's small, I'm sure the price would be more than I could afford!

"How much is the little donkey?" asked Mrs. Beaton.

"I would be happy to sell him to you for a shilling," said Hal.

"A shilling? So cheap?" said Mrs. Beaton. "Is he on his last legs?"

"Not at all," replied Hal indignantly. "He's in perfect health and will probably live a long and happy life."

"But a shilling! At that price I can't even bargain with you," objected Mrs. Beaton.

"A shilling?" said Hal. "Who said a shilling? I said five shillings!"

"Five shillings for that bit of bones who probably won't last the night?" said Mrs. Beaton, frowning. "He's not worth more than tuppence!"

"Three shillings, then," countered Hal, "but only because you're such a good customer."

"Half a shilling and no more!" replied Mrs. Beaton, thoroughly enjoying herself.

"You drive a hard bargain, Mrs. Beaton, and that's no mistake. Half a shilling it is, but there is a slight matter to be discussed.

"And what would that be?" asked Mrs. Beaton.

"The donkey does not belong to the clan. He is my own, personal property. We have been together for some time. Excuse me for just a moment."

Grace watched as Hal walked over to the donkey, placed his hand on the animal's head and gave him a vigorous scratch behind the ears. The donkey leaned into Hal's hand and nodded his head.

"If I didn't know better," thought Grace, "I would think they were having a conversation."

Hal stroked the donkey's back with affection. Then he returned to Grace and Mrs. Beaton.

"Balthazar says that he is willing to live at Emrall Vale," said Hal, "on one condition. If you buy him, I must come along too. I can serve as your stable master."

Grace looked at Hal, shocked.

"What do you mean?" she asked, confused.

"About my coming along with him?" asked Hal.

"No!" Grace fairly shouted. "What do you mean by, "Balthazar says …? Can you really talk to him?"

"I have the gift of the horse," replied Hal. "I don't talk to animals in the way I talk to people, but I can hear their thoughts and communicate with them."

"How wonderful!" sighed Grace. "I wish that I could do that with Blackie, Bronwyn and Boy."

"Maybe someday you will," replied Hal.

"Mommia said," began Grace, and then she stopped. She wasn't sure if what Mommia had told her about the animals talking at midnight was a secret.

Hal smiled at her and then turned to Mrs. Beaton.

"What do you think?" he asked her.

"We have no money to pay you for your labor," Mrs. Beaton said. "As our stable master, you will be taking care of our three, old, very lazy and pampered beasts as well as the donkey. That's a lot of work!"

"A roof over my head — surely there's a little room in the stable — and my meals, and half a shilling a month for my labor will be more than enough. Balthazar and I may be moving on in a few months. Will you have me and my donkey?"

Grace had been following this exchange in amazement. This handsome man was to be their stable master? A little voice in her head whispered, "In the summer, perhaps he'll work with his shirt off when he's mucking out the stalls. Wouldn't that be a treat to see?"

Grace was appalled. She'd never had such a thought in her life! Well, at least not when she was awake! Her dreams over the last year, as she thought more and more of finding her own true love, were something over which she had no control. "Right!" she told herself. She had no control over her dreams. And some of them had been quite disturbing. And delicious!

Meanwhile, Mrs. Beaton and Hal seemed to be looking at one another assessingly.

"Just to be clear," she said, "You and the donkey will come to live with us at the estate. You will act as our stable master for room and board and half a shilling a month."

"Exactly," said Hal.

"I have one demand," said Mrs. Beaton.

"Yes?" asked Hal.

"I cannot have you sleeping in the barn in this cold weather. It's barely warm enough for the beasts. Truth be told, I would bring them into the house if I could think of where to put them on the coldest nights. The house is very large. You must agree to sleep in one of the guest rooms with a working fireplace."

"Oh no!" objected Hal. "That wouldn't be right."

"How about if we call you the stable master/footman?" suggested Mrs. Beaton. "You could be responsible for laying and lighting the fires in the house. You will take your meals with us in the kitchen. And you will sweep the fireplaces."

Hal was startled by this arrangement, but not because of Mrs. Beaton's suggestion. He knew the manor house on the estate. It was quite large. During his rambles through the woods, he had come across Emrall Vale. He had noticed the dilapidated state of the large manor house. Why were there no men on the premises to see to the heavy work and to protect the women? There was not even minimal staff! The situation was outrageous! Grace's guardians truly had no concern for her well-being. Poor little orphan!

"I will move in with Balthazar after the Faire is over," replied Hal.

"In three days' time. That will be perfect," replied Mrs. Beaton.

A question came into Grace's mind.

"Why did you name him Balthazar?" she asked. "It refers to one of the three wise men in the Christmas story, does it not?"

"It does," said Hal. "The name means, 'Bel, watch over the king.' Bel was an ancient god."

"And you gave him this name because …?"

"It's a long story," Hal replied. "The short version is that there was a time when I needed a trusted friend and Balthazar watched over me.

"Since you're here talking to me, I guess he did a good job," said Grace.

Hal smiled.

"He did indeed. And I expect that he will continue to do so."

"And I swear to protect you, Grace" he silently vowed. "You are my intended bride. I will guard you with my life!"

From the corner of the paddock, Hal heard Balthazar bray in agreement. A new adventure was starting for both of them.

A traveling carriage

CHAPTER ELEVEN
In which Hal begins to bring Emrall Vale back to life.

After much discussion, Mrs. Beaton and Grace had prepared the former butler's quarters for Hal. The butler, when there was one employed at Emrall Vale, had a suite of rooms on the opposite side of the kitchen from the housekeeper's quarters.

The two women aired the room and got rid of the cobwebs. They put fresh linens on the big bed — the former butler was over six feet tall — and polished the table in the butler's pantry. Grace chose one of her favorite paintings of Emrall Vale, and she and Mrs. Beaton hung it over the fireplace in Hal's new bedroom.

The day Hal was to move in, Grace gathered some fir branches and arranged them in a large jar. She placed this on the slightly battered table next to Hal's bed. Mrs. Beaton decreed that the room was good enough for the king himself. Grace had laughed. The idea that Hal would be in residence at Emrall Vale gave her a slight fizzy feeling, as though she had sipped hard cider.

Shortly after Hal had settled into his new home, Grace noticed a change in the atmosphere that surrounded Emrall Vale. It seemed like a grey fog had lifted. Everything around her seemed to be bathed in soft, pink light.

"This is very strange," thought Grace. "It's almost mid-December, the gloomiest time of the year. Why do I feel like it's spring?"

Hal found that he was very happy in his new quarters. Balthazar was also happy, enjoying having new roommates in the stable. Originally, Grace had planned to put Balthazar in the stall next to Boy. Balthazar had told Hal that he would prefer the stall next to the stallion.

"Why?" Grace asked, when Hal had proposed the change.

"They're both stallions," Hal had replied.

"Men!" said Grace, but she had agreed to the change.

Juno was pleased with the new addition to the family. She had decided that Balthazar needed a mother. The first night he arrived, Juno left the warmth of her bed in the kitchen ear the fire and slept with Balthazar. Over the next week, Juno transferred some of her treasures into the stall: an old stuffed rag doll, a ball of string and a length of faded blue ribbon. When Hal brought these new arrangements to Grace's attention, she transferred Juno's bedding and water dish to the stable without comment.

Life was good. Hal had appointed himself the estate's unofficial steward. He quickly realized that there was too much work for one man to do if the estate was to be properly cared for. After considering a number of different options, he paid a visit to Alexandru. Hal suggested that perhaps there were some boys in the clan who needed work to do.

Alexandru admitted that ever since the Ravenal clan had stopped traveling, some of the boys were drifting into mischief. Doing chores on the Emrall Vale estate would allow them to work off their excess energy.

Thus, it was that within a week after this conversation that the staff at Emrall Vale expanded to include three gardeners, two stable boys, two woodworkers, two men of all work and three young women eager for the adventure of working somewhere away from their mothers' constant scrutiny. The girls set about cleaning all the rooms that had been shut up since Grace's parents' death. They also took on the responsibility of looking after Grace's bedroom and Mrs. Beaton's suit of rooms. So as not to put a strain on the Emrall Vale resources, all the Ravenal workers brought their own food with them for a mid-day meal.

When he first proposed this plan to Grace and Mrs. Beaton, they were reluctant to accept "charity." But when Hal presented his scheme as a form of apprenticeship, they softened. Hal explained that, by permitting the young people to come to Emrall Vale and work on the estate, Mrs. Beaton and Grace would be helping the Ravenal clan. Mommia and Alexandru wanted the young people to learn new skills.

Hal did not reveal to the women that he himself was paying the young people for their labor. He had begun to draw a stipend from the earldom's estate and could easily afford the expense. Hal knew that if Mrs. Beaton and Grace ever found out that he was paying a wage to the workers, they would refuse to let them work on the estate. They were both very proud and independent women. He admired that about them, but they truly needed help. If ever there were two women who were deserving of help and protection, it was Grace and Mrs. Beaton.

The expansion of the Emrall Vale staff meant that Hal was relieved of the burden of making repairs in the house, cleaning the windows in the bedrooms and the parlor and working in the garden. One day, when walking the grounds to make a list of projects to be undertaken, Hal discovered a carriage house. Within, there were several beautiful carriages that had fallen into disrepair.

Next to working with horses, Hal loved fixing things. He decided to take on the project of restoring the carriages to their former elegance. He was especially drawn to a large traveling carriage. "Wouldn't it be wonderful to drive Grace and Mrs. Beaton to church in this rig," he thought and smiled. He would begin repairing the traveling carriage at once.

One of the highlights of Hal's day was when Grace visited the barn for her daily visits. Now that Balthazar was living in the stable, she included him in her afternoon distribution of apples. Hal made sure to be present when Grace arrived. As he worked quietly in a corner, he listened to what she said to all the animals. It seemed as though they were her only confidants.

"What a brave and lonely soul," he thought. His love for Grace grew stronger with each visit.

To Grace, it seemed as though, wherever she looked, Hal was there. He was always in her thoughts. Every day, when she was selecting apples for her visit to the barn, she would wonder, "Will Hal be there? Will I see him today?" She walked around in a state of fizziness, as though butterflies were fluttering around in her stomach. Before mealtimes, which Hal shared with Grace and Mrs. Beaton, Grace had to talk sternly to herself so that she could calm down enough to eat.

"Really!" she thought, "This is too silly! I've got to calm down. He's just a man! His names don't even begin with an L or a P!"

To her dismay, thoughts about Hal would intrude at the most unlikely times. Like in the bath. Or when she was getting dressed in the morning. Or undressed at night.

"What would it be like to be married to a man like Hal?" Grace wondered. So big! So competent! So handsome! And his hands were so strong!

Ten days before Christmas, Grace began to prepare for her midnight meeting with the animals in the barn. Ever since her discussion with Mommia, she had been working out each detail of her plan. There would be some expenses involved in acquiring everything she would need. Grace wanted to pay for all the items herself.

She had a little green silk draw-string bag that had belonged to her mother. Each year, Mrs. Beaton gave her a shilling for her birthday and a new hair ribbon. Grace put her birthday shillings into that bag, wrapped it in an old piece of canvas and hid it below a board under her bed. It lived happily there with her cache of Christmas shillings.

On rare occasions, Grace needed a little spending money. The household bills were paid by her trustees. Mrs. Beaton had a cash box for household items. When she needed a new ribbon, or when she went on a local outing, like the recent Winter Faire, Grace would take a shilling out of her birthday bag.

The needs on her purse for her Christmas ritual was different to her. She was determined that she would use some of her Christmas shillings to purchase the items she needed. She began to make a list.

Blackie was partial to a warm bran mash with a sprinkling of oats. The bran and oats would need to be purchased, as they weren't normal supplies. Bronwyn thought that raisins were a gift of the gods. Mrs. Beaton usually bought raisins for her Christmas pudding, but the pudding had been made weeks ago and set aside to season. Grace would have to see if there were any left or if raisins would need to be purchased too.

Boy loved sugar. Mrs. Beaton controlled her sugar stores very carefully. But surely, thought Grace, there was enough for a little treat for the faithful pony. If necessary, she could purchase a small cone of sugar.

Juno loved anything that swam in the water. Grace could get a piece of fish from the cook at the Hungry Dragon. And then, of course, there were the ribbons to be purchased.

Grace reviewed her list: Bronwyn, Blackie, Boy, Juno. Oh! Balthazar. She wondered what the little donkey would like. Grace would have to ask Hal. Of course, that would mean she would have to tell him why she wanted to know.

"Well," thought Grace, "In for a penny, in for a pound. The worst thing he can do is laugh at me!"

It was late afternoon, close to dusk. At this time of day, Hal was usually doing something in the barn prior to settling the animals down for the night. Grace put on her warmest cloak and walked out the kitchen door and across the kitchen garden path to the stable. She was looking down and watching her footing. The stones were slick with a thin glimmer of ice. She didn't want to fall. As she made her way across the well-worn path, she heard a man singing. Grace looked up and what she saw took her breath away.

Hal was standing on the highest step of a ladder, tacking a rope of fir to the edge of the sagging stable roof. He was singing "Hark the Herald Angels Sing," with great exuberance. The sight transfixed her. She stood absolutely still, watching him at his work. It was like hearing the familiar song for the very first time.

Grace moved closer to the stable, mesmerized, as twilight deepened. Some slight movement alerted Hal to her presence. He stopped singing and turned to look at her. His face beamed with joy.

Grace gasped. "Is it possible," she asked herself, "for someone to actually steal the breath from one's body?" It was an oddly pleasant, unfamiliar sensation. The world around her dimmed and she slowly began to sink to the ground.

Hal was off the ladder in a moment and running to catch her. He managed to get to Grace just before her head hit the stone path. Cradling her in his arms, he carried her to the shelter of the barn and perched on a bale of hay in front of Bronwyn's stall.

"Lady Grace!" he cried. "Whatever is wrong? Are you ill? Speak to me, dear!" As he held her, he slowly rocked back and forth. Grace, who felt like she was in a very pleasant dream, sighed and snuggled more deeply into Hal's muscular arms. She liked the rocking. The rocking was good.

"Grace," said Hal in a whisper. "Speak to me." Somehow the "lady" was no longer necessary.

Grace looked up into Hal's dark, worried eyes. It seemed to her, in that moment, that all her happiness existed in there.

"I never want to leave his arms again," she thought, happily. Grace noticed that Hal smelled of an enticing mixture of hay, horses, fir and him. The scent made her feel like she was enveloped in a soft blanket of all that was good in the world.

"This is heaven. This is forever," whispered a little voice in her mind.

"Kiss her, you dolt!"

Hal heard the slightly feminine, but definitely horsey voice of Bronwyn in his head. Since coming to Emrall Vale, he had become attuned of the voices of his three new charges.

Bronwyn was a lovely mare, but very bossy. In this case, however, she was absolutely right. He bent his head and placed his lips gently on Grace's forehead with the lightest pressure. He thought he heard Bronwyn snort. Obviously, a kiss on the forehead wasn't what she had in mind. Horses were very straightforward in their amorous pursuits.

Humans, reflected Hal, needed to approach these things with a little more delicacy. Grace hadn't responded to his kiss. He looked down at her. Her eyes were closed. Her breath was soft and even. She had fallen asleep! She had fallen asleep in his arms!

Hal didn't know whether to be honored by Grace's trust or mortified that he had been reining in his deep feelings for her as he cradled her in his arms. Feelings that she didn't seem to have for him, if being in his arms made her go to sleep.

"Crazy human!"

Balthazar's raspy voice with just a hint of Irish in it sounded in Hal's mind.

"Any animal with four legs can see that she's in love with you! Why d'ye think she fainted? Yer handsome masculinity atop that ladder gave her a start, that's fer certain! Yer too much man fer yer own good!"

Hal laughed. He could always count on Balthazar to put him in his place. Carrying Grace, Hal walked over to Balthazar's stall and scratched him behind his ears, just as he liked.

"Thank you for putting me straight, old man," he thought to the donkey. Balthazar made a sound that Hal knew was his laugh.

Grace stirred. Hal looked down at her. She opened her jewel-toned blue eyes and looked up into his. He stood quietly, cradling Grace in his arms. She stirred.

"I think you should set me down," she said softly. "I'm really alright, although I'm not quite sure what happened."

"It's the magic of the season."

Hal heard the bass voice in his head. It was Blackie. The stallion considered himself a wizard out of the tales of King Arthur.

Hal set Grace on her feet while keeping a hand on her shoulder.

"I'm holding her just to make sure she's steady," he explained to himself. Hal heard Boy's derisive chuckle. Boy had no use for anything that was not completely straight forward.

Grace looked around the barn. She saw that there were fir and cedar ropes decorating the stalls and drew in a deep breath. The normal, warm smells of hay and animals were enhanced by the crisp, pungent odor of the evergreens.

"It looks lovely in here," she said to Hal. "I'm sure that all the animals appreciate your efforts to share the season with them."

"I hope so," said Hal. He hesitated, then continued. "They have certainly been giving me enough directions about what they wished me to do!"

"What a lovely gift!" said Grace. Then, making a decision she continued,

"Mommia told me that on Christmas Eve midnight, animals speak in the human tongue. She said that those whom animals favor are blessed with the ability to speak with them."

"Yes, that is true," responded Hal, "but why did Mommia tell you that?"

Grace felt warmth in her cheeks. Was she blushing?

Hal thought it was the sweetest sight he had ever seen. He desperately wanted to pull Grace into his arms and kiss the redness away, whatever that meant! He really was in a bad fix, he thought to himself.

"I feel silly telling you about this," said Grace.

"Please," said Hal sincerely, "there need never be secrets between us. Why did Mommia tell you about the animals talking?"

Grace took a deep breath.

"My parents died in a carriage accident when I was very young. I never really knew them. Mrs. Beaton has treated me kindly all my life, but it was not like having my own parents love me because I was theirs. I always felt lonely.

"When I turned 14, I became aware that boys might be more than just other people."

Her blush spread to her delicate neck. Hal thought that Grace, blushing because she was talking about becoming aware of her womanhood, was the most compelling sight he had ever seen! He wanted to pull her into his arms and kiss her until all she could think of was him.

Grace went on with her story.

"I began to think about what it would be like to have someone of my own, a person I would love and who would love me. Then I would never feel lonely again. I asked Mrs. Beaton how I could find such a person. It was then that she told me about what she called 'the birds and bees.'"

Grace laughed at the memory.

"I asked her if I was a bird or a bee! She gave me a cookie and told me to get about doing my lessons! However, after that, I began to think seriously about who my true love would be.

"Molly, a girl in the village, was getting married. I asked her how she knew that the man she was marrying was her true love. She told me that she had peeled an apple without breaking the peel at the last harvest. She had thrown the whole spiral over her right shoulder. She had asked Mommia for help. When they examined the peel together, they saw that the peel had fallen in the shape of the letter O. Mommia explained the name of her beloved would begin with an O.

"Sure enough, a couple of weeks later, a handsome peddler came to the village. All the girls were smitten with him. His name was

Owen. Molly knew that he was hers.

"When Owen left to finish his travels, he promised to come back for Molly. Many of the adults told her that she was a fool to believe him, that the word of a peddler couldn't be trusted. She remained steadfast in her love and her belief in him. And he did return! Right before the New Year! He courted her for a month and then proposed.

"What happened to them?" asked Hal, enchanted by this story of love.

"Owen gave up his traveling ways and bought a tidy cottage in town. It turned out that he was the son of a rich merchant. He had been peddling to learn about the world of business. He was very well educated, so he and the vicar opened a school for the village children. He and Molly are very happy and have three children.

"Ever since Mary told me about the tradition of the apple peel, I have been trying to divine the name of my own true love in that way."

"So, you do it every autumn?" asked Hal.

Grace hung her head.

"I do it every month," she confessed. Her eyes were fixed on the ground in front of her.

"I'm here!" thought Hal. "You'll never have to peel an apple again!" He desperately wanted to gather his future wife into his arms and cover her sweet face with kisses. But this was not the time. Not yet. Mommia had told him that he would know when it was the right time to declare himself.

"What is the letter of your true love's name?" asked Hal gently.

"I'm not sure," confessed Grace. "Most of the time the spiral doesn't look like any letter. Sometimes I cast more than one peel to make sure the letter I think I see is correct, but the letters never agree."

"When was the last time you did this?" asked Hal.

"Right before the Faire," said Grace. "The letters were clear that time, but they were different. One was a P and one was an L."

"Aha!" Hal thought to himself, "And I am Harold Neil Picton, the Earl of Langafel! Won't she be surprised on our wedding day?!"

He couldn't help himself from teasing the future Countess of Langafel.

"His name might be Peter then," said Hal, "or Paul. Maybe Lawrence? Or maybe the letters stand for your true love's last name, or even his title?"

"You're silly!" smiled Grace shyly, "but very kind to humor me. Most men don't usually believe in such omens."

"Ah," said Hal, "but I'm not most men. Remember, I can hear horses and donkeys talking."

Grace looked him full in the face and gave him the most radiant smile he had ever seen. He would do anything, anything at all, he thought, to make her smile at him like that again. He would give all his worldly goods to see that smile every morning upon waking.

"You are a lovely man," she said, and then her cheeks reddened again. She began to feel warm all over. What was it about this man that made her blush so much? She never blushed. In fact, she couldn't remember ever blushing before. Looking at him she thought, "Wouldn't it be wonderful if he was my own true love? But his name doesn't have an L or a P in it! Could the apple peels be wrong?" Her thoughts were interrupted by the sound of the kitchen bell. Mrs. Beaton would ring it when Grace was outside. Dinner was ready. Where had the time gone?

"Come," she said to Hal. "It's time for dinner."

She impulsively reached out her right hand and he took it in his. They walked toward the kitchen together. Grace thought, "My hand is little and his is big, but together they feel just right."

Ribbons galore

CHAPTER TWELVE
*In which Lady Grace
and Hal share some secrets.*

"I must go into the village today," announced Grace at breakfast the next morning. "I was going to walk but the weather looks a little threatening." Turning to Hal, she asked, "Do you think that Boy might be up to pulling the pony cart? It would make the trip so much easier."

"Boy has been far too pampered," replied Hal. "It's time he got a little exercise and remembered his responsibilities. I will make sure that the cart is ready and waiting for you whenever you wish to go. Would you like my escort? I have some errands in the village myself."

"Thank you so much," said Grace. "I would enjoy your company. I thought I would go right after breakfast. I don't know how long the weather will hold. It looks like snow."

"So it does," said Hal. "Snow seems to be in the air, but I think it will hold up until the afternoon."

An hour later, Grace and Hal were on their way to the village. Hal was driving, although Grace could have handled the reins herself. Grace noticed that Boy seemed to have no problem pulling the cart. In fact, she thought, there seemed to be a spring in his gait. Grace mentioned the pony's new attitude.

"Boy seems happy to be pulling the cart," she said to Hal. "Did you say anything to him?"

Hal chuckled.

"I told him that it was time for him to stop slacking off. I reminded him of his duty to you, who treats him with such kindness and love. I also suggested that when he returned home, he might find some beer in a warm mash. It seems that he loves beer.

"Gelding ponies are very simple beings," continued Hal. "They love their creature comforts. Beer seems to be his. Boy told me that your father made sure to give him a pint of beer every Sunday after church. After your father's death, there was no more beer."

"How did you find out?" asked Grace.

"I heard Boy muttering about it to himself. Ponies do a lot of muttering. There are rarely other ponies for them to talk to, and very often the horses in the stable ignore them. Blackie and Bronwyn are more companionable, but Boy acquired the habit before he came to Emrall Vale. He still does it, usually as he's slipping off to sleep."

"It must be wonderful to understand animals," said Grace. "I hope that I'll be able to talk to the animals in the stable on Christmas Eve."

"What did you just say?" asked Hal.

Grace clapped her hand over her mouth. Had she really just said that?

Hal waited for her answer. The silence grew between them. He concentrated on driving the cart, waiting for Grace to speak.

Finally, she broke her silence.

"I guess it's alright to tell you," she said, "since you probably already know about this and we were talking about it yesterday. Mommia said that animals talk in human speech on the Christmas Eve at midnight. She said that if I did certain things to show respect for the animals in the barn, they might speak to me."

"Why do you want to speak to your animal friends?" asked Hal.

Grace paused so long that Hal thought she might not answer him. Finally, she turned and looked at him assessingly.

"Promise me that you won't laugh or tell me that I'm being silly," she said.

"Never," replied Hal in a serious voice.

Grace heard his sincerity. She took a deep breath and then explained.

"Mommia said that the animals could tell me the name of my own true love."

"Oh, my sweetest, dearest love," thought Hal. "Your own dearest love is sitting right next to you," but he said nothing.

Grace misinterpreted his silence.

"You think I'm silly?"

"Not at all," Hal hastened to reassure her.

"You see," Grace continued, "My trustees want to marry me off to some man they like so that they can control my money."

"You know about that? Hal asked.

"Mrs. Beaton showed me their letter. Of course, the trustees didn't say anything about my money. They said that since I couldn't have a come out, they had arranged a suitable marriage for me. Mrs. Beaton thinks she knows who it is, and she doesn't approve. Besides, I want to marry for love.

"My trustees said that I won't meet my future husband until the day of the wedding! That can't be a good thing, can it? And we're going to go away to Ireland right after the ceremony. What do you think of that?"

What Hal thought was that his Grace was the sweetest young woman in the world. And the bravest.

"And you want to know the name of your intended because?" he asked.

"Well, if it's anyone in the village, I will ask him to marry me as soon as possible. Because I'm not of age, we would have to ask my trustees for permission to marry. They won't give it, so we won't ask them. We'll have to go to Gretna Green and marry over the anvil."

Hal laughed.

"My parents did the same thing. I'm told they were very happy together," he said.

"You were told they were happy? Didn't you know them?"

"No," said Hal. "My mother died shortly after I was born. My father died a few days after that. I was raised by a couple in the village where they lived."

"I'm so sorry," said Grace.

"I was very happy with my adoptive parents," said Hal. "When I was 18, they told me the true story of my birth. My mother was related to the Ravenal clan. I came to them to become acquainted with my kin."

"And your father?" asked Grace.

"That's a story for another time," replied Hal. "Look, here we are in the village. I'll leave Boy and the cart at The Hungry Dragon. Then I have some shopping to do. Where will you be going?"

Grace blushed. She knew that there was no fireplace nearby, but if felt like there was! She thought, "I have to stop blushing. It's absolutely silly!"

"I have to buy ribbons," she said in as normal a voice as possible. Then she added softly, "For all the animals, even Juno. For the ceremony on Christmas Eve."

She looked at Hal, expecting him to know all about the ritual. He looked back at her, puzzled.

"You know," she said. "Mommia said that I have to braid their manes with their favorite color ribbon. Then I have to ask them for forgiveness for anything I have done to hurt them."

Hal was amused, but kept his face solemn. He had never heard of that ritual and suspected that Mommia had created it just for Grace. Braid their manes with their favorite color ribbon indeed! He wondered what Blackie would make of that! But Hal never questioned Mommia's wisdom. If this was a ritual she had crafted for Grace, then it was what Grace needed to do. He certainly wasn't going to tell her that Blackie, Bronwyn, Boy and even Balthazar wanted to talk to her and had a lot to say! Keeping his own council, he asked, "Would you like me to help you pick out the ribbons?"

"Oh, would you?" she asked, relieved. "I'm afraid that I'll get all the wrong colors and that the ritual won't work. And you know them so well. I won't ask you to tell me what their favorite colors are. That would be cheating. But perhaps you could steer me away from colors they would hate?"

"Every word out of her mouth is a blessing," thought Hal. "She is so honest and brave. What a magnificent countess she will be."

After leaving Boy in the care of the hostler at The Hungry Dragon, Hal and Grace walked to the mercer's shop together. There was a rainbow of ribbons on display.

"Look at this brilliant red!" said Grace. "Wouldn't Bronwyn love this?"

"Actually," said Hal. "Horses can't see oranges, reds or purples."

"I never knew that!" replied Grace. "What colors can they see?"

"Yellows, yellow-greens, blues and white. They can't tell the difference between red and green, and they can't distinguish shades of orange and red."

"Thank you so much for telling me," said Grace. "I would have chosen reds and pinks for Bronwyn."

"Bronwyn is a real lady," said Hal. "She would have appreciated the gesture and not complained."

"Mommia said that part of the ritual was showing the ribbons to all the animals, and figuring out which color they like best. I want to please all of them. And I can't imagine what color Juno will prefer."

"Cats seem to be attracted to blue and yellow," said Hal. "We had a ginger kitten when I was growing up. He always snatched my mother's yellow shawl off the line when it was drying. He would make it into a nest and sleep in it. Mother had red and green shawls as well, but he never touched them. After the third time mother retrieved the shawl, she relented and gave it to him. He's an old guy now, but he still sleeps with that shawl."

Grace laughed.

"I'll get yellow and blue ribbons for Juno, then," said Grace, "and see if I can determine which one she likes best."

"That sounds like a good idea," said Hal. "As for the other animals, I won't tell you which of them will like which colors, but I suggest that you buy two different shades of yellow, yellow-green and blue. And maybe two white ribbons.

"Thank you for your guidance," she said.

Hal made her a formal bow.

"It is a pleasure, my lady," he said. He took her hand and kissed the air above it.

Grace curtsied and then giggled.

"My lord," she said.

Hal escorted Grace into the mercer's shop. They spent the next hour selecting ribbons. As Grace was paying for her ribbons, she noticed that Hal was buying several that were red and green. She wondered if they were gifts for Mommia. Or maybe they were gifts for a young woman whom he admired. That thought made her feel a little ill.

"Silly!" she admonished herself. "He's free to admire

whomever he wishes!" Grace found that she didn't quite believe those words. She waited for Hal in front of the mercer's store. He came out, smiling, and looked up at the sky.

"I think the snow will hold for a few more hours," he said. "Would you like to have luncheon at The Hungry Dragon?"

Grace had never eaten at the tavern. She willingly agreed. Then an unwelcome thought intruded. Would it proper for her to dine with a man in public without a chaperone? Why had she never thought about this before?

Mayo – a wise woman's companion

CHAPTER THIRTEEN

In which Hal relates the story of The Hungry Dragon.

The main room of The Hungry Dragon had a long bar on one wall and a number of rough-hewn tables placed fairly close together around the room. There were a few people sitting at the tables. Hal greeted the proprietor, who greeted him by name. Hal introduced Grace.

"Lady Grace," said the proprietor. "It is a pleasure to see you here. The Hungry Dragon is known for its hospitality. Are you waiting for Mrs. Beaton to join you?"

"Mrs. Beaton was unable to accompany us on our trip to the mercer's this morning," said Hal. "Lady Grace is hungry and tired. We wondered if we could have a quick meal. Perhaps your wife might chaperone us?"

"Of course, of course," said the proprietor. "Since it is mid-day, she will chaperone from the kitchen. Let me settle you in this comfortable table in the corner.

Once they were settled, a young woman Grace had seen at church, came to the table. Hal greeted her with a smile.

"Good afternoon, Tilda," he said, smiling. "What is on the bill of fare today?"

Tilda smiled back and recited the day's offerings.

"The game pie is especially good here," Hal said to Grace. "Would you like that?"

Grace had never eaten game pie, but she felt adventurous. She nodded in assent.

Hal ordered for both of them, and Tilda gave a little curtsy before hurrying off to the kitchen.

Grace noticed that Hal had smiled again at Tilda. Did he have to smile at every single woman in the world? She wondered. Why did she care?

The food came quickly. The game pie was served with beets and endive and a fresh loaf of bread served with butter. Grace thought it was the most delicious meal she had ever eaten.

Immediately upon that thought, she felt disloyal to Mrs. Beaton. Mrs. Beaton's meals were always well prepared, filling and good tasting. But she had never made anything like the game pie Grace had just eaten. It was a revelation! The pastry was rich and flaky. The filling of the pie had spices in it that Grace had never encountered before.

"On the other hand," thought Grace, "maybe what makes the meal so special is the company." She had never eaten a meal alone with a man before! And such a handsome, attentive man. He made sure that all the food was to her liking and that her glass of lemonade was kept filled. Hal kept up a steady flow of interesting conversation.

For dessert, Hal suggested apple dumplings with custard, which came out of the kitchen smelling delectable. Grace took a bite as soon as her portion was placed in front of her.

"This food is heavenly," said Grace. "The pastry is light as air. The apple inside is so tender. And the caramel and custard …". She ran out of words to express her delight.

Grace was suddenly aware that all of her desert was gone. She looked up at Hal.

"Did I really eat all of the dumpling?" she asked him, slightly puzzled.

"And half of mine!" said Hal, laughing. "I've never seen anyone enjoy apple dumplings so much!

Grace bowed her head, slightly embarrassed. Hal reached across the table and, putting his forefinger under her chin, he raised her face so that they were looking directly into one another's eyes."

"Don't be embarrassed," he said softly. "You were so lovely, I was transfixed. When you finished your own dumpling, I didn't want to break the spell. I slipped the remaining part of my dessert across the table underneath your descending fork. It was a delight to see you so happy."

Grace's embarrassment gave way to a shy smile.

"Please don't tell Mrs. Beaton," she said. "I wouldn't want to make her feel bad. But that is absolutely the most extraordinary thing I have ever eaten!"

Hal laughed, thinking, "If you are so lovely."

To snap himself out of his reverie, Hal changed the subject.

"Do you know how this tavern got its name?

Grace frowned.

"I don't think so," she said. "I've never heard anyone speak of it. Do you know?"

"Actually," said Hal, "I do. A few years ago, our camp was visited by a very old man who had some horses he wished to sell. He had grown up here, but had left as a young man to see the world. He had only recently returned to find his family estate in ruins and the horses, for which the estate had always been known, sadly neglected. He hoped that we would buy them and treat them well.

"The man shared a meal with us. As we broke bread, he told us something of his history.

"He explained that, growing up in the village, he had always been fascinated by the picture of the dragon on the sign of the tavern. One day, he asked the oldest man in the village to tell him why the tavern had chosen that picture and name. This is the story as he related it to us."

A long, long time ago, there was a peaceful little village much like this one. Everyone was happy and no one was ever hungry. When food was scarce, neighbors shared what they had. When food was abundant, neighbors shared their bounty. It had always been that way. The villagers believed that it would always be thus. And life went on, and it was good.

One day, a very wealthy lord and lady rode into the village on fine horses with a large retinue of soldiers. They pulled up to the small tavern that served the village. The tavern had no name. The locals called it "the tavern." The lord and lady entered the establishment and demanded that their entire entourage be fed with the finest food available.

It was a time of scarcity in the village. The couple who owned the tavern had very little food on hand. They were afraid to offend their wealthy customers, but they barely had enough food to feed their own family, although there was plenty of ale and cider. Everyone in the village knew this, so everyone ate in their own homes and only came to the tavern to imbibe the fine drinks on offer.

As in all villages, it took only a few minutes for word of the tavern owners' problem to come to the attention of all the people in the area. No one wanted their village to be shamed before these powerful visitors.

"Every person in the village gathered as much food as they could and brought it to the kitchen entrance. The goodwife was overwhelmed. With tears in her eyes, she accepted these gifts from her friends and neighbors, vowing to compensate them in kind when she could. But all that those generous people would say was, "For the honour of our village will the strangers be served the best we have to offer."

While the tavern keeper's wife was busy cooking, the proprietor was handing around mugs of ale and cider to his guests. At first, they refused his offerings, saying that they only drank the finest wines. However, the ale and cider brewed in those parts was the finest to be found in all the kingdom. Perhaps in all the world!

The tavern keeper encouraged his guests to sample his beverages. After the first sip, they all agreed that, while the ale and cider wasn't fine wine, it was certainly an adequate beverage. They continued to drink it.

Finally, the meal was ready. The tavern keeper's wife and some of her neighbors began to bring out platter after platter of good, wholesome food. There were pies of all descriptions, bowls of tender turnips lovingly cooked in butter, bright red beets and loaves of freshly baked bread served with sweet butter. When the lord and lady saw this food, they laughed.

"Where is the chicken with mushrooms and a sauce of sweet cream?" asked the lady scornfully?

"What is that foul odor?"

"This is food we give to our pigs!" one of their servants shouted.

"This is not proper food for our lord and lady!" said another servant, disdainfully.

The lord and lady stood up and brushed the platters of food, so lovingly donated and so carefully prepared, to the floor. Their servants trampled the food beneath their boots so that it was not edible by man or beast.

The lord and lady angrily walked out of the tavern, leaving no payment for the drink, the food or the service. As they were leaving, they said to their servants, "This is truly a place that has no right to exist, so shabby is its hospitality. When we are gone, burn this tavern to the ground!"

"The servants all roared their approval at their employers' command. None of them saw a stooped old woman sitting in a dark corner of the tavern, or the enormous, golden-eyed calico cat beside her. She was the wise woman of the village. The cat, Mayo, because she was born in May, was the wise woman's companion. Some people in the village believed that Mayo was a wise woman in her own right. She always seemed to turn up when a difficult situation was brewing.

"The woman had been observing the lord and lady's bad behavior and their disdain for the good food served to them. They needed to be taught better manners, she decided.

Rummaging around at the bottom of the sack she always carried with her, she pulled out a black, white and red striped candle molded in the shape of a dragon. She showed it to Mayo, who, if anyone was looking, would have seen her nod her head as if in agreement to an unspoken question.

The wise woman placed the candle on the table before her. She lit it and began to circle the flame with her hands. She sang a strange melody. The words were in a language no one recognized. Over and over, her hands circled the flame as it burned brighter and brighter. Daylight began to fade, even though it was still early afternoon.

The soldiers, who were planning how they would burn down the tavern, saw the light begin to dim. Rather than just destroy the tavern, they had decided to burn down the whole town and were making their plans.

The villagers also saw that the sky was darkening. They stood in their doorways and noticed something truly miraculous. Although the daylight was fading faster and faster, there was a soft golden glow as though the purest candles were burning in each of their homes. The miracle, was that no candles were lit in the entire village because it was just past mid-day.

Although it was summer, the day suddenly seemed unusually cold. A howling tempest came from the north. The houses began to sway, although none shattered. A high-pitched sound like a crying babe was carried on the wind.

"It's the Hungry Dragon," some of the older villagers whispered to one another. "She is awakening!

The day grew darker and colder. The crying of the wind reached a feverish pitch.

The soldiers were becoming extremely nervous. A feeling of great menace seemed to be entering the village. Just when the darkness seemed almost impenetrable, the captain of the soldiers said, 'This is not natural! This is a sign from the heavens above! Mount up! We will follow our lord and lady, we will be on our way! We must not burn this tavern or hurt this town!'

Some of the soldiers, who were looking forward to making mischief, began to object, saying 'Our lord and lady told us to burn down this miserable tavern! Who are you to countermand their orders?'

"I am your leader,' said the captain, "and a man who knows when there is witchcraft afoot! Do you think that this darkness and this cold and this crying wind are natural? Don't you men have the sense you were born with? We are being warned not to harm one blade of grass in this village!"

"You're crazy,' shouted one of the soldiers. "Just a superstitious old man! Get out of the way, you coward. If you can't follow our lord's orders, I'll do so!" Some of the soldiers shouted encouragement at the rebellious soldier, while others murmured amongst themselves.

Just at this moment, the wise woman and her cat came out of the tavern. They were both surrounded by an aura of soft, golden light.

"Listen to your captain,' she said. Her voice was very soft, but all could hear it clearly. "Your captain is a wise man. He is the survivor of many battles because he understands the signs of the heavens. The darkness, the cold and the crying wind are all warnings. A great power is approaching, which considers this village its own.

"Your evil thoughts and bad deeds have disturbed the rest of the Hungry Dragon, the one who protects this hamlet. You are lucky. She always sends warnings to evil-doers before devouring them.

"The Hungry Dragon knows the evil that is in your hearts. Your wicked thoughts have disturbed her slumber! She is coming! If you don't leave immediately, she will descend and there will be nothing left of you but a stray memory of your presence. Go!" The wise woman commanded, "and quickly so that you may avoid your doom! Should you be spared, you must never return! The Hungry Dragon has a long, long memory, and her vengeance is eternal!'

As the old woman finished her warning, Mayo seemed to grow in size. Her fur radiated out from her body like shards of multi-colored glass. Malevolent rays of light shot from her eyes. The light pierced the darkness with a shimmering green iridescence. The cat's hissing could be heard throughout the village, angry and menacing.

The soldiers were all terrified. For a moment they stood stock still, as if frozen. Then, an eerie sound came from Mayo's throat. It sounded like a dying soul in Hell.

That was enough for them! Almost as one, the soldiers vaulted on their horses and rode out of the village fast as they could. All the villagers watched them go. When the dust of the last horse could no longer be seen, the darkness lifted and the town was filled with clear daylight.

The villagers rushed to the tavern and surrounded the wise woman and Mayo. They thanked them both for saving their village.

"It was the Hungry Dragon that saved the village," said the wise woman. "Mayo and I were only her handmaidens."

The tavern keeper and his wife joined the crowd, tears streaming down their cheeks. Everyone was talking at once about the miracle they had seen. The tavern keeper cleared his throat, dried his eyes and spoke.

"'Our wise woman, our Mayo and the Hungry Dragon have saved us all. In their honor, from this day forth, this tavern will be called The Hungry Dragon. The name will remind us that, in a time of great peril, we stood together.

"We may not always be able to wake the Hungry Dragon to drive away evil doers, but we can always, and must always, depend on one another. Our spirit of community will make this village safe and strong forever."

All the people in the village cheered. The local artist said, 'I will paint a beautiful sign for the tavern. In the corner, with your permission,' he said, bowing to the wise woman and to Mayo, 'I will paint a picture of both of you." They bowed their heads in agreement.

The local scribe said, 'I will write the names of every person in the village on the back of this sign. Thus, no one will ever say, in some far off day, 'It's only a story. It didn't really happen.'

"Yes,"said the tavern keeper's wife. 'That is a very sensible idea. This day and what we have learned must be passed on to every generation.'"

Hal stopped speaking.

"Is that the end?" asked Grace.

"Yes, it is," said Hal.

"But is it true?"

"Of course it's true," responded Hal. "Come. Let's go outside. I'll show you the remnants of the names on the back of the sign."

Grace's face glowed with wonder. She had never heard such a story in all her life. She and Hal walked outside. He pulled a bench under the sign and helped Grace onto it. Then he very carefully rotated the sign so she could see the back.

She was astonished. There was, in fact, a list of names written in fading black ink on the back of the sign! Grace thought this was the most amazing thing she had ever seen. She looked down at Hal, smiled broadly and then laughed.

"Thank you," she said. "I have never seen such a miracle in all my life!"

"And I," thought Hal, "have never seen such a miracle as you in all my born days."

Instead of giving voice to that sentiment, Hal said instead, "It's time we were getting home. It's gotten colder while we were inside. The snow will start soon."

They walked over to the pony cart. Boy had just been hitched to the traces. Hal walked up to his head and scratched him behind the ears.

"Thank you, Boy, for agreeing to pull the cart today. We'll get back much more quickly than if we were walking. I'll see that you get a very special mash when we get back to the stable."

Grace came close to Hal and said in a very soft voice, "Please give him some beer."

Hal nodded his head, once more overcome by the kindness of his beloved's heart.

They reached the stable at Emrall Vale just as the first snow-flakes began to fall. Grace looked up to the sky and stuck out her tongue to catch a falling flake.

"Oh, stallions and mares!" thought Hal, watching her. "This innocent young woman is going to be the death of me! Snowflakes on her tongue, for pity's sake!" He watched her for several minutes, admiring her beauty while longing to gather her into his arms.

Mrs. Beaton had seen the pony cart drive up to the stables and came out of her kitchen. She took in the tableau that Hal and Grace made in the falling snow and smiled to herself. Things were progressing just as she and Mommia had hoped.

"Grace! Hal!" she called. "You'll catch cold out there! Come in and have some hot chocolate and gingerbread cookies. I just made a batch in the shape of bunnies!"

"I'll help you settle Boy down first," Grace said to Hal.

"No," responded Hal. "I can do that quickly. Once he's fed, I'll join you and Mrs. Beaton. My father taught me that animals should be cared for and fed before humans because they can't do it for themselves."

"Your father sounds like a wise and caring man," said Grace.

"Yes, he is," replied Hal. "And my mother. Even though they did not give me birth, I love them, and my younger brother and sister as well. They are truly my family."

Grace smiled a little sadly.

"You're very, very lucky," she said. "And you have your Ravenal family as well."

"You'll have your family, too," said Hal. He noticed that Mrs. Beaton had returned to the kitchen. Impulsively, he drew Grace into his arms.

"You'll have your family, too," he said softly into her snow-kissed hair. The snowflakes glistened on her dark locks.

Time seemed to stand still for Grace. Hal was embracing her. What was he saying about her having a family? She was confused, but for the moment, she was blissfully happy. He was so warm! She had been getting chilly, standing still as the snow fell. Now she was as warm as though she was standing before a blazing fire. And safe. And loved.

"And loved?" she thought? "Did I really think that?"

Hal pulled away from Grace and said, "Its cold. Go into the house. I'll be there soon."

He looked down into her face and smiled. She smiled back.

"Go," said Hal, giving her a little push.

Grace went.

Mistletoe

CHAPTER FOURTEEN

*In which Lady Grace receives
a special gift that compels
Hal to kiss her.*

Every day after that, when Grace went to the barn, she brought
the ribbons with her. When offering the horses and Balthazar their
apples, she talked to them as usual. However, more than ever
before, Grace confided all her hopes and dreams to her equine
companions. After they had enjoyed their snack, she would show
each of them the different colored ribbons and try to decide which
they liked best.

Grace had narrowed down the choices. Blackie liked white and
yellow. Bronwyn enjoyed the light blue ribbons. Boy disdained
everything other than a shiny blue-green ribbon. Balthazar didn't
seem to like any of the ribbons. She also showed the ribbons to
Juno, who had shown a preference for an elegant blue velvet ribbon.

Each day, Hal watched as Grace spoke with her four-footed friends. He noticed how much they all loved her.

On the day before Christmas Eve, Grace came to Hal, frustrated.

"I don't know what to do," she told him. "Balthazar has rejected each ribbon I've presented. He acts as though everything I've presented is unworthy of him!"

Hal laughed. "Come with me," he said, leading her towards Balthazar's stall. Juno was curled up in the corner as usual.

"Balthazar," he said to the donkey as he reached over and scratched the beast behind the ears, "Why are you putting on such airs before your friend Grace? She is trying to please you."

Balthazar shook his head and made a snuffling noise.

Hal looked at Grace and said, "Balthazar has a very noble lineage. He maintains that he is of royal donkey descent. He thinks he should have a ribbon for his mane that is more splendid than everyone else's."

"My!" said Grace. "What a revelation! I had no idea!"

Was it her imagination, or did Balthazar seem to preen at her words?

"I think I might have the very thing in my box of special treasures. I'll be right back."

Grace returned in a few minutes holding a length of something that glistened. She held it up to show Balthazar and Hal. It was a long ribbon made of cloth of gold. It gleamed in the few stray rays of fading daylight.

"This was a ribbon that my mother wore in her hair when she made her come out," Grace explained. "One of the few memories that I have of her is when I was about five. She showed me how to wind this ribbon through her curls. I begged her to put it through my curls and she did so, even though the ribbon was much too long. We laughed. She told me that when I was 18 and ready to make my come out, I would wear it in my hair and dance all through the night with handsome young men."

Grace was lost in thought for a moment. She sighed.

"My mother was so beautiful."

"She couldn't have been more beautiful than her daughter," thought Hal.

"I begged her to let me sleep with the ribbon and she agreed," continued Grace. "The next day, she and my father went away and I never saw them again."

She was quiet for a moment, remembering her loss.

"I took the ribbon and put it away. I vowed that I would wear it one day, but I never have. Perhaps it's fitting that this noble animal wear it in his mane."

She looked at Balthazar and showed him the ribbon.

"What do you think, Balthazar?" Grace asked. "It's one of my most prized possessions."

Balthazar sniffed the ribbon and then angled his head so that the gold material was draped over his neck. Grace thought that he might be smiling.

"I guess this meets with his approval. What do you think?" Grace asked Hal.

"Indeed," said Hal. "It will make him look noble and majestic on Christmas Eve."

Grace was pleased that she could make Balthazar smile.

The next day was Christmas Eve. Grace followed all of Mommia's instructions. She curried all four of her friends and brushed Juno until her fur shined. She wiped all the animals down with a warm, damp cloth, dried them and braided their manes with the ribbons each preferred. She fed them their favorite meal. Bronwyn seemed especially happy with her raisin mash.

Grace didn't see Hal at all that day, but she knew he was

around. All the stalls had been swept, the water buckets scrubbed and filled with fresh water and each of the animals had fresh hay.

When all her duties in the barn were finished, Grace went to the kitchen and bathed in the tin tub that she and Mrs. Beaton kept in a little room next to the pantry. She dried her hair in front of the kitchen fireplace. When her hair was dry, Grace went up to her room, brushed her hair, secured it in a knot and put on her very best dress.

The dress was dark-green silk with silver bells embroidered around the neckline and the sleeves. It had belonged to her mother. The year before, Mrs. Beaton had made it over for her as a birthday present.

Grace instinctively reached for the box in which she kept her mother's silver locket. When she opened the lid, she saw that the box was empty. Then she remembered that she had given the locket to Mommia. For just a moment, a feeling of loss came over her.

"It's Christmas Eve," Grace said to herself. "This is going to be a very special night!"

She looked into the small mirror on her dresser and thought that she looked very grown up. For just a moment, she imagined that she saw her parents behind her, smiling. She reached forward, as if to touch their beloved faces. Then she heard the dinner bell and hurried downstairs.

Hal was sitting at the kitchen table speaking to Mrs. Beaton, who was wearing her best gown, covered with a long, crisp, white apron. Hal was dressed in his Sunday best. Grace thought that he looked very handsome. He was wearing a green silk waistcoat. A thick gold chain for a pocket watch was threaded through a buttonhole.

"That's a handsome chain," said Mrs. Beaton.

Hal reached into his pocket and pulled out a gold pocket watch that was attached to the chain.

"This is one of the few possessions I have that belonged to my

father," he said. He flicked it open. Inside the cover was a miniature of a beautiful young woman with dark black hair. "This is a
picture of my mother," he said.

"She was beautiful," Grace said.

Hal detached the chain from his buttonhole and handed the
watch to Grace,

"Why don't you keep this for now," he said, "so that you'll
know when it's time to go out to the stable."

Tears came to Grace's eyes. What a thoughtful, kind man
he was.

"Thank you," she said. "I was beginning to wonder how I
would know when it was time to leave, other than to race into the
parlor and check the clock every few minutes."

Mrs. Beaton chuckled.

"This is a much better idea," she said. "Why don't you put it
beside your plate on the table." Grace followed her friend's advice.

"What a special night this is," said Hal, looking at both
women. "A very happy Christmas Eve to you both." He paused
for a moment and looked at Grace with shining black eyes. "May I
say, Lady Grace, that you look quite beautiful tonight. But there is
something missing."

Hal walked over to a shelf near the kitchen door and took
down a small box. He examined it for a moment, and then returned
to the kitchen table and handed it to Grace.

"A remembrance for the season," he said.

Grace was surprised. She had received very few gifts in her
life. That it came from Hal made it even more special. When she
opened the box, she found a small bundle of mistletoe and holly
bound together with a green ribbon. There were several hair pins
tipped with chips of a sparkling red mineral.

"It's beautiful," she said.

"Let me help you with it," offered Hal.

He took the hair ornament and attached it with the pins and

ribbon to the knot at the nape of Grace's neck. Then he turned her head to the right and to the left to make sure that the ornament was placed correctly. He looked straight into Grace's eyes and said, "Perfect!"

"Oh!" said Mrs. Beaton. "Mr. Ravenal! Look!"

She pointed to Grace's hair ornament.

"There is mistletoe in my dear Grace's vicinity! Quick, you must kiss her or bad luck will descend upon our house."

"I've never heard of that custom," said Hal. "That failing to kiss a young lady in the proximity of mistletoe is bad luck. However, I'm not from these parts. I will happily honor your custom," he said, with a courtly bow. "I would never want to cause ill fortune to fall on this house and its inhabitants."

Hal put his hand under Grace's delicate chin and lifted her face up to his. Then he lowered his lips and slowly and carefully kissed her.

Grace's eyes fluttered shut. The light pressure on her lips made her feel slightly dizzy. Could it be an invitation to something more? Could this be love? She wished that the kiss would never end.

It did, however. After all, Mrs. Beaton was standing right there, watching the two of them.

The rest of the evening was taken up with wonderful food and storytelling. Hal encouraged Mrs. Beaton to tell stories about her life growing up in nearby Wales. From time to time, Grace checked the pocket watch, anxious to make sure that she didn't lose track of the time.

Hal told stories of his foster family and his brothers and sisters. Grace amused Mrs. Beaton and Hal with her ideas about how each of the animals in the barn might sound when then talked to her. She was sure that Bronwyn would have a very aristocratic accent!

At 10:30, Grace went to fetch her coat, a warm wool hat and a scarf. It was time to go to the stable to speak with her friends and perhaps discover her future. She was very nervous. As she was opening the kitchen door, she turned and said to Hal, "Can you come with me?"

Hal shook his head.

"These rituals are best performed alone," he said. "But don't be worried. All the animals love you. This is a special time for you and for them."

"Everything will be fine," Mrs. Beaton assured her.

Grace wished that she could believe them. If everything was going to be fine, why did it feel like bats were flying around in her insides? She took a deep breath and said to herself, "I can do this." Then she closed the kitchen door. As she walked to the stable, she wondered what this night would reveal. Would she discover the name of her one true love?

Bronwyn – queen of the stable

CHAPTER FIFTEEN
*In which the animals,
finally, speak.*

The stable was warm compared to the weather outside. Grace stood inside the big doors and looked around. Hal had lit a number of oil lamps and hung them all around the stable. The room was filled with a warm glow.

Grace inhaled deeply. The intoxicating smells of the stable were blended with the scent of cedar and pine. She wondered if the animals liked the aroma as much as she did. Soon, perhaps, she could ask them. If they liked it, perhaps she would keep fir and cedar in the stable all year long.

With a shock, she remembered that she might not be in residence in Emrall Vale very much longer. A deep sadness descended as a tear rolled down her cheek.

No sadness. All good.

Grace started. The words had come into her mind with a slight purring sound. Was Juno speaking to her? She looked around, but didn't see the cat. Was she curled up in Balthazar's stall? It wasn't yet midnight. How could Juno speak to her?

Juno was special, though. Perhaps she could speak before midnight because she was Juno. Everyone knew that Juno was one of a kind.

Grace's sadness lifted. She decided not to think about the future. She would concentrate on what she had to do now.

Grace walked into the center of the stable. She positioned herself so that she could see all of her friends. Then she took a deep breath and began.

"Good evening," she said. "I have come to ask you to forgive me for anything I have done this year to make unhappy. Please know that I would never hurt you intentionally. I love you all. You are my family.

"It is only recently that I learned of this custom of coming on Christmas Eve to ask for your forgiveness. I hope that, in years to come, I will act in such a way that there will be nothing to forgive.

"I have tried my best to visit you every day and to give each of you a treat. However, I realized today, when I brought your special mashes, that perhaps an apple a day is no longer a treat. Perhaps some of you would prefer a carrot or something else.

"If you grant me the opportunity to speak with you a little later, please let me know what you would like me to bring to you. I will try my best to do so."

Bronwyn whinnied. It sounded like she agreed.

Grace had said everything that was in her heart. She stopped talking. The night was very still. She had left the pocket watch on the table and she didn't know what time it was. Suddenly, through the woods, she heard the ringing of the church bells in the village. She counted each peal. Ten. Eleven. Twelve. It was midnight. The time when animals could speak in the human tongue!

She waited and wondered. Should she say something? Were

there rules about how to conduct a conversation with animals? Why hadn't she asked Mommia this important question?

Suddenly, she heard a rich, deep voice singing. At first, she thought it was Hal, but then she knew it wasn't he. His was a baritone voice. This voice was much deeper. It had a kind of raw sound, as though it was out of practice. She listened closely, trying to make out the words. She thought that the voice might belong to Blackie.

"The gypsies came to our good lord's gate
And oh but they sang sweetly!
They sang sae sweet and sae very complete
That down came the fair lady.

Grace thought that she heard a high, purring soprano, singing a melody. Another voice joined in, a light tenor. Grace turned toward Boy and saw that his mouth was moving.

"O come with me, says Johnie Faw,
O come with me, my dearie;
For I vow and I swear by the hilt of my sword,
That your lord shall nae mair come near ye."

A fourth a sweet alto, joined in. Bronwyn.

"And when our lord came hame at e'en,
And spier'd for his fair lady,
The tane she cry'd, and the other reply'd,
She's awa' wi' the gypsy laddie!"

Blackie continued.

"Gae saddle to me the black, black steed,
Gae saddle and make him ready;
Before that I either eat or sleep,
I'll gae seek my fair lady."

Boy finished the song.

"The gypsies came to our good lord's gate
And oh but they sang sweetly!
They sang sae sweet and sae very complete
That down came the fair lady."

There was a very high-pitched purred cluster of notes that seemed to ascend to the very rafters of the barn as the song ended.

When there were no more verses, Grace clapped her hands, enchanted.

"That was so lovely," she said. "I had no idea that you all liked music. I'll come and sing with you every day! I love music also."

'Tis a clue, lassie," said a somewhat braying, nasal voice.

"That must be Balthazar," Grace thought. "What type of clue was that?" she wondered. Aloud she said,

"Thank you so much for singing such a lovely song."

Do ye want another clue? asked Balthazar.

Don't pretend that you aren't here to seek our counsel, said Bronwyn.

We know that you want information about your own true love, said Boy.

Blackie grumbled.

Human nonsense, love, he said. *A lot of much ado about nothing! Mares don't need love! They need good shaking!*

Grace was a little shocked by Blackie's statement, but she didn't object. By a stallion's lights, he was exactly right.

You big hypocrite, said Bronwyn. *All that nuzzling that you do when we're out in the pasture! What do you call that?*

Preparing for shaking! responded Blackie. *It always helps to get a mare in the mood first. Makes the shaking better!*

Grace thought that she heard Bronwyn stifle a laugh.

There was a sigh. Grace realized that it was Boy.

"What's wrong, Boy?" asked Grace.

I've never been in love, said Boy.

"I love you, Boy," said Grace.

You're a good girl, said Boy to Grace. *You always were, even as a tyke. You was always gentle and kind.*

So give her a clue, said Blackie.

Boy shook his head.

Don't know any clues, he said.

"The apple peel ritual said that the man who is my own true love has a name that starts with an L and one that starts with a P," said Grace. "I don't know anyone with names that begin with both those letters. Do you?" she asked.

An L and P, said Bronwyn. *Don't you know a man with a name that begins with P?*

"You mean Hal?" asked Grace. "He doesn't have a name that begins with an L or a P!"

L, P, said Balthazar. *It's all human silliness. What's in a name? Maybe your own true love doesn't have a name at all,"* he continued.

A sweet, rumbling soprano broke in. It sounded like the voice Grace had heard when she had first entered the stable. Juno.

It's not the name that counts! It's how he smells. If he smells right to you, he's the one. Don't worry so much about letters and such. Get a good sniff of his neck and his hair. That will tell you the truth.

Grace laughed.

How does the stable man smell? asked Juno.

"Hal?" replied Grace.

Yes, said Juno. *What does he smell like?*

Grace thought for a moment. Then she said, "He smells delicious, like leather, fresh air and something else I can't name."

Delicious is good, purred Juno.

What about the name? asked Boy. *Names are very important. Every being has a name.*

Well, said Balthazar, maybe your true love's name is a secret.

"A secret?" said Grace. "What do you mean?"

Maybe he doesn't know his real name, replied Bronwyn.

Or maybe he needs to hide his name, said Balthazar. *I don't tell everyone that I'm a direct descendent of a royal donkey. Can you imagine what would happen if I told everyone that? They wouldn't leave me alone!*

But you do, said Bronwyn.

Maybe no one would care, said Boy with a rather snide edge to his voice.

Grace heard a threatening growl from Juno. She was protecting her little Balthazar.

Gentlemen! shouted Bronwyn. *This is not the time to brangle. Today is a holy day.*

Humph! muttered Boy.

Blackie let out a sharp snort.

Back to business, he said. *Our Grace has two clues. Give her another, Bronwyn. Make it a good one!*

Welllll, said Bronwyn. *How's this?*

In the forest, in the wood,

It was there the young man stood.

His golden lass, her face was bright,

Of her he now dreams every night."

Oh! That's excellent! Bravo, Lady Bronwyn, said Balthazar.

Indeed, agreed Blackie. *Quite el-e-gant.*

"I don't know what it means," said Grace, getting a little frustrated. She believed that her friends all knew the name. Why wouldn't they tell her?

How about this? asked Balthazar.

The Earl of L rode out one night, to give his dear some wooing,

She was the pearl of his delight, just made for love and cooing.

He said, "Oh loveliest of all, my own true love are you,

And I am he, I'm by your side, if only you would see me."

There was silence in the barn. Then Blackie said, *That's not a proper poem, you know, old man. It doesn't rhyme or scan. Ha! I just made a poem!*

Not much of one! I know my poem wasn't perfect, replied Balthazar, *but no one ever recited Shakespeare in my presence. I don't have yer sophisticated way with words. However, it's an excellent clue. It's all true, if only our little miss would see it! It tells her everything she wants to know!*

Smell! That was Juno's soprano voice.

Grace was ready to scream. She loved her four-footed friends. She truly did.

"I really don't understand any of your clues," she said, permitting her exasperation to show. "You all obviously know who my true love is. Why can't you just tell me his name, or where I can find him?"

Ah, deary, to tell would be cheating! Our being able to talk on Christmas Eve has rules you see, explained Bronwyn.

Quite right, said Blackie. *Quite right. Rules. Mustn't break the rules.*

I say we break the rules, said Boy. *We shouldn't make our Grace suffer so.*

We're not making her suffer, responded Bronwyn. *We're helping her the best way we can. You know what will happen if we break the rules, Boy.*

Boy sighed.

I know. I know. We'll never be able to use human speech again. Well, so what? he muttered.

If one of us breaks the rules, we will all be punished, Bronwyn chided him. *You may not care, but think of how Blackie would feel. He so loves to quote Shakespeare on Christmas Eve.*

And I really like the singing, said Balthazar. *Music is food for the soul.*

Grace could hear Boy grinding his teeth in frustration. She walked over to him and stroked his mane.

"It's really alright, Boy," she said soothingly. "I wouldn't want any of you to suffer on my account. Rules are important. Everyone has to follow some rules. I'll work hard to figure out the clues. I'm sure they're excellent and will help me a great deal."

Of course you'll figure out the clues, said Bronwyn. *Your true love is so close you could touch him. Maybe Hal can help you find him,* she said, slyly. *He's a very clever young man. And handsome, too.*

Bronwyn ... said Blackie. His voice had a strange, solemn, almost threatening sound.

Yes, Blackie, she sighed

The apple peel never lies, purred Juno. *My ancestors knew all about the apple peels.*

Why don't you give our Grace a really good clue? Something Shakespearian, perhaps, said Bronwyn.

Very well, said Blackie, clearing his throat. *If you insist. Something better than Shakespeare. A verse almost all my own.*

"My true love's hair is not gold,

My true love's eyes are not blue,

Love looks not with the eyes

but with the mind,

to have and to hold.

Oooh, sighed Bronwyn. *Partially quoting from a Midsummer Night's Dream! So appropriate for Christmas Eve.*

I remember when Grace's father and mother would come into the stable on Christmas Eve. They loved talking to us, said Bronwyn. *When we told them that we loved poetry, your father began to read and perform Shakespeare. After you were born, they brought you with them. Your mother would sing our favorite old songs. She had a beautiful voice, like an angel. Your father was a wonderful actor.*

Tears began to course down Grace's cheeks. Even though her friends couldn't tell her exactly what their clues meant, they could tell her about her parents. What a wonderful gift that would be. Perhaps hearing stories about her parents was more important than learning the name of her own true love. She was sure she would be able to figure out the clues by herself. She had only this one night to learn about her parents.

Why are you crying, my dear? asked Bronwyn. *Have we made you sad talking about your parents?*

"No, not at all," replied Grace. "Indeed, I was wondering if you would be willing to tell me more about them. I was so young when they died. I hardly knew them. You all knew them better than I did. Except Balthazar, of course."

Your parents died? asked Boy. *No! It can't be! I thought they went away on a very, very long trip like humans do. Why, I expect them to return any day now! Surely they're coming home to you, if you only wait a little while longer. They can't be dead! Dead means never coming back! I don't want them to be dead.* He kicked up his hind legs in agitation.

Bronwyn sighed. *Oh, Boy,* she said softly. *We've told you this many times, but you never remember.*

I don't want to remember bad things, muttered Boy.

Grace rushed over to Boy's stall, flung open the door, and threw her arms around his neck. She was sobbing.

"You are the best, most wonderful Boy in the world," she mumbled into his mane. "I love you so much."

Now, now, little Grace, said Bronwyn. *There is no need for tears. Surely your parents are always with you in your heart. And wherever they are on their journey, they are certainly looking out for you. Why, they have sent your own true love to you!*

Bronwyn, rumbled Blackie. *Rules!*

Yes, but look at the poor thing, said Bronwyn. *She's crying!*

Of course we'll tell you about your parents, said Blackie.

Yes, of course, said Bronwyn. *Balthazar is lying down in his stall. I'm sure he'd like it if you went over and cuddled up next to him while we tell you about your parents.*

Yes, do just that, said Balthazar. *I didn't know yer parents, but I can tell ye stories about Hal. Ye'll like that, won't ye?*

I'll cuddle with you too, said Juno, a soothing purr in her voice.

That is a very good plan, said Boy. *I have stories to tell too. I can tell you about the day that I first met you and how your father put you on my back. You were a wee bit of a thing.*

"I'd like that very much," said Grace. She gave Boy one last big hug and went over to Balthazar's stall. He was lying in state with his cloth of gold ribbon woven into his mane.

Grace knelt down next to him and got comfortable. The donkey felt very cozy and warm. Juno glided over, circled three times and then cuddled up next to Grace. Grace put her head on Balthazar's side. She could feel his heart beating and it was very soothing.

Grace began to listen as Blackie, Bronwyn and Boy told her about her parents.

"This is the best Christmas present anyone could give me," she thought.

Grace listened to her friends talk about her parents and about Hal all night long. As the sun began to inch up over the horizon, she nodded off to sleep with the rumble of their voices deep in her heart.

When Hal came into the stable later that morning, he found Grace sleeping deeply, cuddled up against a lightly snoring Balthazar. Hal bent down and gently took Grace in his arms, trying not to wake her. She snuggled up against his chest, a sweet smile on her face.

"Thank you," he thought to all the animals as he carried his future wife up to her bedroom.

Juno, who had sensed Hal's approach, followed them. As he had drawn closer to her girl, Juno had smelled how much he loved her. She knew what happened when a male of any species smelled like that. Although Juno had no use for human ideas about when it was right to mate, she knew that her Grace must be treated with respect. She followed them into the house.

Hal drew back the covers of Grace's bed, laid her down and covered her. He placed a light kiss on her cheek and lingered for a moment, nuzzling her neck.

Juno approved. Nuzzling, knowing the right smell, was good. Then Hal straightened up and quietly left the room. She sighed a little meow of relief. Juno could have attacked him if she had to, but, she admitted to herself, she hadn't wanted to do so. She was getting a little old for such exertions. And really, this human man Hal was a good man. But he needed to declare himself soon. Juno remembered the evil-smelling men at the stable. Time was running out.

Will you take me as your husband?

CHAPTER SIXTEEN
*In which an elopement
is planned.*

Grace slept well. In her dreams, she had been galloping across
rolling hills. A handsome man, who looked like Hal, was riding
toward her. Suddenly she awoke. It was past noon, and she was
surprised to find herself in her bed. She washed and hurried down
to the kitchen. Mrs. Beaton was putting the finishing touches
on their Christmas dinner, which would be served at four that
afternoon. Seeing her, Mrs. Beaton came over to Grace and gave
her a big hug.

"Happy Christmas, my dear one," she said. "It's good to
see you awake. I thought that just this one time, we could miss
Christmas morning services. You had a long and late night. I hope
that it was everything you wished it to be."

"I'm sure the vicar will understand if I tell him I stayed up late
on Christmas Eve," said Grace. "I surely would have dozed off

during the sermon and that would hurt his feelings," thought Grace.

"Come and break your fast with some raisin scones and chocolate," said Mrs. Beaton, leading Grace to the big table.

"Chocolate!" said Grace. "What a treat!" Mrs. Beaton rarely bought drinking chocolate because it was so expensive.

"And there is lovely raspberry jam and Devonshire cream!"

Grace sat down at the table with a light heart.

"Was the experience in the stable everything you wished?" asked Mrs. Beaton.

Grace looked at her friend, puzzled. What did she mean? Then it all came back to her. The horses. Balthazar. Their singing. Their clues. Their stories about her parents and Hal. It seemed like a beautiful dream.

"Oh!" she said. "It was the most wonderful and strange night of my entire life! And a Christmas gift beyond compare! But would you mind if I wait to tell you until we're having our dinner with Hal? I want him to hear the story too."

At four o'clock, Grace, Hal and Mrs. Beaton gathered around the table in the breakfast room for their holiday dinner. Once again they were dressed in their finest clothes, but each had added a special Christmas Day touch.

Grace was wearing the hair ornament Hal had given her. In addition, she had wound a new green ribbon through her hair. Would Mrs. Beaton insist that Hal kiss her again because of the mistletoe? Grace hoped so.

Mrs. Beaton wore the gold and onyx broach that Grace's mother had given her their last Christmas together. She wore it on special occasions. Whenever Grace saw it, she felt her mother's presence in the room.

Hal was wearing a shiny white stud earring in place of his everyday gold stallion. On the lapel of his jacket was a sprig of mistletoe tied with a red ribbon. When Grace saw the mistletoe, she wondered if that was an invitation for her to kiss him.

The table was set with care. On Christmas Day, Mrs. Beaton brought out the family's best table cloth and what was left of the family's precious china and silver. The table was decorated with fir branches and a bowl of white and pink Christmas roses that Mrs. Beaton grew in her kitchen garden. In the center of the table was a silver bowl with a large pineapple in it, surrounded by oranges.

Grace exclaimed in surprise when she saw the centerpiece. Although their local market occasionally carried oranges, they were still a treat. But it was the pineapple that surprised her. She had heard of them but had never actually seen one. Pineapples were so expensive, that only the wealthiest London hostesses could buy them to eat. For households with a smaller budget, pineapples could be rented as a decoration for a centerpiece.

Mrs. Beaton smiled at Grace's reaction.

"The pineapple and oranges are a gift from Mommia. They are from the Ravenscrofft conservatory. Mommia said that she wanted you to have a special treat on this day so that you would always remember it."

"I always shall," said Grace. "This is the most remarkable Christmas, ever!"

"Let us begin our dinner," said Mrs. Beaton.

They started the meal with a white soup, a recipe that had been handed down in Mrs. Beaton's family from mother to daughter since time immemorial. With it, she offered a plate of tiny mince pies filled with beef, raisins, spices, apples and secret ingredients.

Before Christmas, Mrs. Beaton had baked dozens of miniature mince pies to distribute to their neighbors on Boxing Day. Most families ate mince pies for each of the 12 days of Christmas to insure good luck for each month of the year. The mince pies of Emrall Vale's kitchen were highly prized.

Looking at the platter of mince pies on the table, Grace thought about the story of The Hungry Dragon. The villagers always shared what they had with one another. It seemed that, besides the names on the back of the tavern's sign, there were other remnants of that long-ago event that still endured in her village. It gave her a warm feeling to be part of such a special place.

As they ate their meal, Grace told Hal and Mrs. Beaton of her experiences in the barn at midnight. From time to time, Grace saw that Mrs. Beaton had tears in her eyes, especially when Grace spoke of the stories the horses and Boy had told her about her parents. From time to time, Hal seemed to have the need to clear his throat. Finishing her story, she said,

"The horses, Boy, Balthazar and Juno are very dear, but I wish they had told me the name of my true love. Balthazar sang a song about the Earl of L. And Bronwyn said that my true love is so close I could touch him! I'd touch him if I knew who was. Bronwyn said that I should ask Hal to help me."

"Animals never lie, especially on Christmas Eve," said Hal softly. "And I would be happy to help you find your true love."

"I really wish they hadn't been so mysterious," Grace sighed.

"What else did the animals tell you?" asked Mrs. Beaton.

"Juno said that the apple peel ritual always works. He must be someone I already know."

Turning to Hal she said, "You are the only man I know. But your names begin with H and R, so it can't be you." Then she whispered to herself, "How I wish it were you."

Hal pretended not to hear and suppressed a smile. His Grace was such a delight. Her heart was pure and true. They would be so happy together.

Grace pushed her chair back from the table and began to walk about in a small circle. After a minute or so, she turned toward Hal and asked, "Is it possible that the animals are mistaken? Perhaps they have their letters wrong. After all, I've never heard that animals could read or spell."

Hal laughed.

"Actually," he said, "horses and donkeys, while they don't actually read, recognize certain words that they see very often. They seem to recognize letters and words that are associated with objects they know.

Grace sighed.

"I don't know what to do," she said. "My trustees are sending a carriage to take me to London in just a few days. My time is running out! If I'm not married to my own true love before the carriage arrives, what will I do? My trustees will force me to marry the man they've chosen."

"Maybe the man they've chosen will be young, handsome and amiable," suggested Hal. "He might even have his own hair and teeth."

Grace scowled at him.

"Even if he's perfect," wailed Grace, "he won't be my own true love. He'll be someone that they can control. I don't care about my fortune, but I want to have a life with a man I can love and respect. And his names should begin with L and P. How can that be a man my trustees have picked so that they can pillage my estate?"

How he loved her, Hal thought.

"If you think that the animals have not been helpful, and you are afraid of being forced into marrying someone you don't think you'll be able to respect," said Hal, "perhaps you should marry me." Then he thought, "Oh lord! I'm an imbecile! That was no kind of proposal. Please don't let her reject me out of hand."

"You?" she said, puzzled.

Was her tone dismissive? What did Grace mean by "you?" Hal didn't respond.

Grace walked over to the window of the breakfast room and looked out over the snow-dusted lawn. It was dusk, but she could see the fir trees of Emrall Vale standing tall and proud in the distance. Mrs. Beaton made herself busy with clearing the table and left the room.

Hal pushed back his chair and walked over to Grace, barely breathing. He was so angry with himself. "Perhaps you should marry me?" That's how he proposed to his true love? "What was I thinking?"

Grace turned around. Tears were rolling down her cheeks.

"Do you really mean it?" she asked. "Would you marry me to save me from my trustees? Since I'm not 21, I need my trustees consent to marry. I won't even be 18 until December 31. My trustees will never give their consent.

"We don't need their consent if we marry over the anvil," said Hal.

If I don't get their consent to marry, we'll have to run away to Gretna Green and marry over the anvil.

"What does that mean?" asked Grace.

"In Scotland, a couple can get married by a village blacksmith," said Hal. No license is necessary. Gretna Green is the first town right over the border. My parents were married in Gretna Green."

"My trustees would probably use the excuse that I married without their consent to withhold even the small allowance they're giving me now. I have my Christmas shillings, but I know that isn't much. I would come to you with nothing but the shift on my back."

"I'd take you without the shift on your back," thinks Hal. He scolded himself for uttering that improper, but quite delightful thought. Then he drew Grace into his arms.

"I've loved you from the moment I saw you, Grace," he said. "You were walking in the woods with Mommia. A shaft of light came through the trees and bathed you in golden sunlight. I stood still. I knew, in that moment, that there would never be anyone else for me but you."

A phrase from the previous night popped into Grace's mind, a part of Bronwyn's clue:

"His golden lass, her face was bright,

Of her he now dreams every night."

Could Hal, even with no L name, be her own true love? For she surely loved him.

Hal knelt down on one knee and continued speaking.

"Please marry me, Grace, please take me as your husband. I love you more than I can say."

"There," thought Hal. "That's a proposal!"

"Oh Hal," said Grace, "You're such a good man. I won't bring anything other than myself to the marriage. You're so good, kind, smart and resourceful. Any woman would be lucky to marry you.

"Are you sure you want to marry me?" she asked. "You could marry a woman with a substantial dowry. You could live in comfort for the rest of your life."

"The problem," said Hal, standing up, "is that I don't want a woman with a substantial dowry. I'm part Rom. Such things are not important to me. I want only you. I swear to you that you will never know a day of want if you marry me. I have some resources."

"I do truly love you," said Grace, "even if you don't have a name that begins with an L.

"Or with a P," added Hal.

Grace looked at him, momentarily surprised. What an odd remark, she thought.

"Despite what the horses said," Hall continued, "maybe you read the apple peel incorrectly. Apple peels aside, do you love me, Grace?"

"You make me feel safe and warm and cherished," she replied. "That can't be an accident. In my heart, I feel that you must be my own true love!"

Blackie's quote from a Midsummer Night's Dream came back to her.

"My true love's hair is not gold,
My true love's eyes are not blue,
Love looks not with the eyes
but with the mind,
to have and to hold."

Hal's hair wasn't gold and his eyes weren't blue, thought Grace. Was that a hint? And "Love looks not with the eyes, but with the mind." Maybe the word mind really meant the heart. The heart knows what is true.

Hal!" thought Grace. "I really believe that the horses and Balthazar were telling me that Hal is my own true love!"

She looked up into Hal's beautiful black eyes, as deep as the midnight sky. She moved closer to him and drew in a deep breath. Juno had said that a man's scent would tell her the truth of her heart.

Hal smelled like love and caring … and safety and children … and home! Juno was right. Grace gently pulled back and looked into Hal's questioning eyes. Grace lifted her hand to Hal's cheek and stroked it gently.

"Yes," she said softly. And then louder, throwing her arms around his neck. "Yes, yes, yes! I will gladly marry you as soon as can be!"

Hal bent down and showered Grace's face with kisses. "How much I love you," he whispered in her ear. "We will be so happy together. I promise you that from the depths of my soul!"

Mrs. Beaton walked into the breakfast room at that moment. When she saw them in their embrace, she smiled and sighed.

"Well now," she said, "That's settled at last."

Grace pulled back slightly from Hal's arms.

"What do you mean, *settled at last?*" she asked Mrs. Beaton.

"Mommia and I have been hoping that you would find one another," said Mrs. Beaton. "We both thought that you were well suited. The wedding should be soon, lest your conniving trustees show up early and surprise us."

"Grace has explained that she doubts her trustees will give her their blessing to marry me," said Hal. "We're going to elope to Gretna Green and marry over the anvil."

"A blacksmith is going to marry us," said Grace.

"They like to be called "anvil priests"," said Hal.

"Quite right," said Mrs. Beaton. "A good plan. When do we leave?"

Hal smiled.

"I had hoped that you would feel that way. It would be very helpful if you would join us to act as chaperone for Grace and also to give her company. I'll be driving."

"Oh, dear Mrs. Beaton," said Grace, "will you truly come with us? It would make me so happy if you were with me on my wedding day."

"You're sure that he's your own true love, even without a name that begins with L?" asked Mrs. Beaton, a twinkle in her eye. All Mommia had revealed to her had come to pass.

"Yes," said Grace. "I'm really and truly sure."

"Excellent," said Mrs. Beaton. "We can both be ready as soon as Hal can make the arrangements."

"We'll leave at first light then," said Hal. "I'll borrow four carriage horses from the Ravenal clan. I knew that there had to be a reason why I was drawn to restoring your traveling carriage. It's now in excellent repair. Nothing will stand between us and a life of happiness, my Grace."

A formidable weapon

CHAPTER SEVENTEEN
In which an L and a P are revealed.

As it turned out, not only Mrs. Beaton, but Alexandru Ravenal escorted the betrothed couple to Gretna Green. When Hal asked for the loan of a team of horses, Alexandru had insisted on coming along to share the driving. He also arranged for one of his nephews to move into Emrall Vale to care of the horses and Balthazar while Mrs. Beaton and Grace were away.

Their party left the next morning, amply supplied with food and drink for the journey. The weather, though cold, was dry. At each stop, Hal made sure to get hot bricks for them all so they could warm their feet.

They pulled into Gretna Green in the middle of the day of New Year's Eve, the day when Grace was supposed to be in London to ready herself for her wedding. Hal and Alexandru were both outside, sitting on the coachman's bench. As they pulled up to a pleasant-looking inn, Mrs. Beaton turned to Grace and asked, "Do you want to get married today, or will you wait until tomorrow, when you've rested?"

"Today, I think," said Grace. "As soon as possible."

And so it was done.

When Hal and his new bride were going into the anvil priest's study to sign their marriage lines, Hal turned to Grace.

"Before we sign our marriage lines and make everything legal," he said, "I have a gift for you. Mommia said that I was to give this to you right after we completed our vows."

Hal put his hand into the pocket of his outer coat and pulled out a small, silver silk drawstring bag. He handed it to Grace.

"What is it?" she asked.

"Mommia said you would understand," said Hal.

Grace held the elegant bag in her hand. It obviously had something in it, but she couldn't imagine what it was. It didn't feel like a ring. Besides, Hal had already given her a beautiful gold ring that had belonged to his maternal great grandmother. He had told her that Mommia had given it to him.

She opened the bag and spilled its contents into her open palm. Then she gasped! It was her mother's silver locket, the one she had given to Mommia on the day that Mommia had told her fortune. Grace was shocked. What had Mommia said when she had taken the locket from Grace?

Grace closed her eyes and recalled the scene, just as it had happened. Mommia had said, "I pledge that one day you will be reunited with it. When you are, you will know that you have found your own true love."

Her own true love! Hal, even without an L name, was definitely, and without a doubt, her own true love. He hadn't married her just to save her from her trustees. He was, really and truly, her own true love! Any lingering doubts Grace might have had floated away as though they were nothing more than a will o' the wisp.

Mommia, and the animals in Grace's stable had been right all along. Hal, who didn't have gold hair and blue eyes, who was a gypsy carrying her away, who saw her in the forest bathed in gold light, was her own true love. She looked up at the dark sky and sighed. Her new life was beginning and she knew that it would be wonderful.

Grace looked up into her husband's face. Their eyes met. She saw the light of love in his eyes. He was hers. She was his. She would never be alone again. Grace felt a stray tear make its way down her cheek.

Hal stepped closer to her and gathered Grace into his arms. With one of his strong, calloused fingers, he gently wiped away her tear.

"No tears my sweet one," he said. "Only laughter." He lowered his lips to hers and gently kissed his new bride. Grace pulled in a deep breath and then sighed, melting into her husband's warm embrace.

"Come," whispered Hal. "Let's sign the marriage lines. We're not officially married until we do."

Hal had a momentary qualm about what was to come when Grace learned of his complete name. Would she be pleased or angry that he'd concealed certain information from her? Either way, the deed was done and he couldn't be happier. Grace was his for as long as they both drew breath.

Shortly after the signing of the marriage lines.

"You beast! You monster! You crawling worm! How could you do that to me? You knew I was worried about the apple peel ritual!"

The newly minted Countess of Langafel, began to beat her laughing husband about the head with her small wedding bouquet of dried white heather. She was both laughing and crying at the same time as her bouquet disintegrated, creating a hail of floral snowflakes.

"You knew how concerned I was that you didn't have an L or a P name and you didn't tell me! I should tear up our marriage lines right now! The Earl of Langafel! And you're rich! Truly rich!"

"Enormously rich, actually," said Hal, smiling broadly.

"Embarrassingly so for a Rom. All my relatives are pity me. However, since it's inherited wealth from my father's family, they are willing to overlook it."

"Beast! Monster!" Grace began to flay her husband again with the remnants of her wedding bouquet.

"You already said that," said Hal, laughing. "Stop! Stop! You're missing the point."

"Which is what, exactly?" asked Grace, exasperated. "That you lied to me? That you hid your true identity?

"That I love you madly," replied Hal. "And that you and Mrs. Beaton will never have a day's worry in your lives! Now that you've married me, your trustees no longer have any part to play in your life. Your money is now in my control, not theirs. And soon it will be completely under your control."

"What do you mean?" asked Grace, diverted by his change of topic.

"When I learned from Mommia and Mrs. Beaton how your trustees were trying to get access to your fortune, I set my man of business on their tails. He and some friends of mine in London are in the process of sorting out your trustees. They'll see to it that all your funds are deposited into a bank account in London in your name. Any money that has been embezzled will be returned to you, although it may take a while to collect it all.

"What about the man they had chosen for my bridegroom? Now that we're married, will he leave me alone?" asked Grace with a worried frown.

"The Earl of Nottingham, "said Hal. "My informants tell me that he has been living well above his means for many years and apparently owes a great deal of money to some extremely nasty customers. He has been letting his creditors know that he will be wedding an heiress at the beginning of the New Year. When the word gets out that the wedding will not come about, England, and most likely Ireland as well, will be much too hot for him.

"Just to make sure that the Earl will not trouble you, I have arranged to assist him in relocating to the Americas."

Grace gazed up at her husband, her eyes sparkling with admiration. He was not only handsome and loving, he had the military instincts of a general! But, she reminded herself, he had lied to her! She stepped away from him, her hands fisted on her hips.

"Harold Neil Picton, Earl of Langafel! Picton! Langafel! A P and an L, just as the apple peel spell, the horses and Balthazar had promised. Why didn't you tell me? You knew how concerned I was about finding my true love."

Hal looked down and examined his boots. Grace thought he looked a little ashamed. "Good!" she thought. There was a pause and then Hal said something very softly.

"I didn't hear what you just said," Grace told him.

Very quietly, still avoiding her eyes, Hal murmured, "I wanted you to love me for myself. Not because some magic spell told you I was your true love."

"The magic of love is the only true magic. It is alchemy. It makes two hearts one."

Grace heard the voice in her mind. There was a warm purring sound behind it. It sounded like Juno's voice.

"I wanted you to love me for myself," Hal repeated.

"Oh Hal," thought Grace. "Oh Hal!" How could any woman resist such a man?

Grace threw her arms around her husband's neck and kissed him with all her might. Even if he was a beast to tease her so, he was her beast. And absolutely and definitely her own true love. She buried her nose in the lovely curve of his neck. He smelled of home. She continued to kiss him until they both had lost their wits - it was the first of many such happy kisses in a long and fulfilling life together.

Everyone needs a journal

EPILOGUE

Lizzie's bedroom at Emrall Vale.
1810
A day closer to Christmas.

Mrs. Beaton closed the book and smiled at her niece.

"That was such a beautiful story," said Lizzie. "But what a surprising ending!"

"Yes," replied her great aunt, "it was!"

"A Lady in Love writes such wonderful books," continued Lizzie. "Mother gave me one of her novels for my last birthday and I couldn't put it down. I've read it three times! Father hinted that there might be another book by A Lady in Love for me at Christmas."

"A Lady in Love certainly does write enchanting tales," agreed Mrs. Beaton, smiling.

"I've read all of her books and they never disappoint. There is always a happy ending and a serious reckoning for the villains."

"Do you think the story is real?" Lizzie asked. "I wish I could talk to animals on Christmas Eve." She yawned. "Perhaps they could give me clues about my future. I'm not sure I really want a husband. They sound like a great deal of work!"

Mrs. Beaton chuckled.

"That they are, my dear," she said. "That they are. But when you get a good one, he's worth the trouble."

She rose from her chair and leaned over her great niece to fluff her pillows and adjust her covers.

"It's time for you to get some more rest." The older woman kissed Lizzie on the cheek and then straightened up, smiling at her.

"Why don't you study the portrait opposite your bed for a few minutes as you prepare for sleep. Perhaps the images will accompany you into your slumber and give you restful dreams."

She left the room, closing the door behind her.

Lizzie had been looking up at her great aunt's sweet face, feeling safe and protected as she did so. She shifted her gaze to the large wedding portrait hanging on the wall opposite her bed. The portrait had been painted by Thomas Lawrence, a friend of the present earl and countess, shortly after they married. It usually hung in the present earl and countess's bedroom. When Lizzie fell ill, her great aunt had the painting moved into Lizzie's room to keep her company.

Lizzie hadn't paid much attention to the painting before. Now she subjected it to close scrutiny.

A young couple, presumably the count and countess of Langafel, were seated side by side on a sofa, looking at one another. They were holding hands as if they would never let go. Each wore a smile of dreamy contentment.

Lizzie examined the count. He was dressed very informally. His white shirt was open at the neck, revealing his bronzed skin. His buff leather breeches looked like they had been painted onto his muscular legs. Lizzie laughed. Of course his breeches had been painted on! The count had a shock of white hair running from his right temple to the back of his neck. It was just like Hal's hair in the story!

The countess was wearing a simple white muslin morning gown. The bodice and the edges of the elbow-length sleeves were embroidered with green rosettes and trimmed with a hint of lace. A thin green ribbon was threaded through eyelets underneath her bosom. She wore a silver heart-shaped locket around her neck. On a small side table next to her lay a blue leather-bound journal.

The foreground of the painting showed a ruby-red Axminster carpet with a blue and gold geometric pattern. Lizzie recognized the carpet as the one that held pride of place in Emrall Vale's formal parlor. She had seen it when she had tea on the day she arrived.

On the carpet, between the count and countess, an enormous calico cat was curled up on a green velvet cushion. Peeping out from underneath the countess's skirt, was the head of a tiny kitten with a black spotted nose. Lizzie recognized the kitten as Novo, the cat who had been her companion since the first night of her visit. The cat who was even now curled up on the foot of her bed, snoring peacefully.

The background of the portrait was very dim, but it gave the impression of a stable with four stalls. Four animal heads could just barely be seen. There was a noble black horse, a beautiful bay, a sweet grey pony and an aristocratic-looking donkey with a gold ribbon worked into its mane.

Lizzie suddenly noticed that there was an object lying on the countess's lap. What was it? She squinted, trying to make out the details. It was a book bound in rose-colored, watered silk. The pages had gold edges. It looked very much like the book that her great aunt had read to her. The countess was cradling the book with love.

"Oh my!" Lizzie thought. "Oh my!" Could it possibly be? She fell back against her pillows. Was Lady Grace Cooper Picton, Countess of Langafel, that wonderful teller of romantic tales, Lizzie's favorite author, A Lady in Love?

The housekeeper in the story was named Mrs. Beaton. Was Lizzie's great aunt Grace's Mrs. Beaton? Lizzie wanted to get out of bed and ask her great aunt if the story was written by the countess. At the same time, it had been a very long day and she was tired. She yawned.

Lizzie contemplated the picture. It gave her a feeling of utter peace and happiness. She yawned and settled deeper into her bed.

You're getting well. You need to sleep.

The voice in her head was loving, with a slight purr. Lizzie felt better than she had in days. She was immensely comforted by the voice that was speaking to her. She had been very ill, but soon she would be well. And Christmas was approaching.

Her eyelids began to close. Just as Lizzie was drifting into sleep, she heard, *We will speak to you after the 12th bell tolls on Christmas Eve. Until then, rest and recover. You will need all your strength for the adventures that lie ahead.*

With a sigh of deep contentment, Lizzie drifted off into sleep.

The End

Until next year.

Thank you!

ACKNOWLEDGMENTS

About a year ago (from the time I'm writing this, in the early summer of 2024) my creative partner and editor, the amazing poet and artist James W. Gaynor said to me, "Why don't you write a series of holiday-themed short stories? We could publish them as you finish them and then produce them as an anthology." Short stories generally run between 3,000 and 7,500 words. In a normal week, I can produce about 10,000 words. "Easy," I thought. I started working on a Christmas story.

It's interesting the things you don't know about yourself, no matter how old you are. I've written three novels of over 100,000 words each. I discovered, in trying to write my Christmas story, that I'm incapable of writing short fiction! It didn't help that Jim, when I turned in my first draft—about 10,000 words — had a list of things he felt were missing that required about another 20,000 words. We decided that I'd make the Christmas story a novella (up to about 40,000 words.)

Guess which writing team can't produce a novella? You know what the problem is? There's just so much to say!

I learned a great deal writing *Midnight Miracle*. I loved writing about the animals, and especially about the cats. (They were Jim's suggestion.) I've never written about animals before and it was great fun to have their distinctive non-human energy surround me and their distinctive voices whisper in my mind.

Getting a book from one's brain into one's hands takes the assistance of a great number of people. I am blessed with the many members of the Nola team. Huge hugs go to Kelly Duke McKinley, our award-winning designer at the shopkeys.com for another beautifully designed book. The cover, in particular, is genius. Thank you so much. Heartfelt thanks also to Peter McKinley, our website director. You keep things going even when I'm caught up in the weeds. I so much appreciate all you and your talented staff at the Shop Keys do to keep the Nola ship afloat.

Many thanks to our proofreader extraordinaire, Jenny Rodriguez — another amazing job!

Figuring out how to illustrate this book was, as my husband Neil would say, "a bear." A special thank you to the extremely talented Madeline McKinley for her heroic efforts in attempting to illustrate this story. In the end, we decided to use a different artistic approach. This was no reflection on Madeline's outstanding work. Clients can be so impossible!

Today, successfully launching a book is all about public relations and social media. I am blessed to be working with two magnificent, talented women, one on each coast. Buckets of thanks to Marla White, Whitehanded.com in California, for her outstandingly successful efforts in providing public relations and promotional support. And unceasing applause for our social media guru, Danielle Snyder, Brightseed Creative, Florida, for creating and managing a brilliant social media campaign. It's amazing how far we've come in such a short time. Thank you also to our Amazon whiz, Ryan Childs, who is our intrepid guide in Amazon land.

I have a secret to share with readers who are not writers. Writing fiction is exciting, exhilarating and more fun than one person should be permitted to have. BUT. Writing can make you extremely crazy. If you want to be a professional writer, it is absolutely imperative to surround yourself with relatively sane people who will make sure you eat regularly, do something other than write once in a while, and who will love you even though all you can talk about is why your heroine is refusing to behave and do what you want her to do. I am blessed with a wonderful network of friends and family who take care of me when I get lost in Regency land.

My head honcho is my husband, Neil, who met me when I was thirteen and who hasn't let me go since then. The words don't exist to tell you, Neil, how much it means to me that you completely support me in pursuing my dream.

My creative partner, editor and dear friend, James W. Gaynor, is the Nola Whisperer. I listen to him and do what he tells me — even when he tells me I have to kill some of my darlings — because he's right 99 ½% of the time. It is such a tremendous blessing to have someone to work with who is so supportive and giving. For everything, Jim/Willie, thank you.

The Bible Explorers, an interfaith group of intrepid adults with a passion for text study, have been my weekly companions for almost ten years. Working with you all gives my life balance and the thrill of discovery. Special thanks to Alan, Ed, Emily, Jim, Liz, Marlene, Rebecca, Rona, Susan, Tamara, Trudy and Zeita.

A special thank you to my family for their love and support. Evan and Cathy, Andy, Ali, Chris and Ava and Justin and Judy, Lior and Ezra. Cathy, I promise that you can read this book without having to peek through closed fingers at any particular page.

Finally, thank you to all my friends — old and new — who read *Anarchy at Almacks* and let me know you enjoyed it. A writer hopes that someone will read the story and find something new and wonderful in it. I hope that this holiday tale will make the dark days of winter a little brighter.

Nola Saint James

How can Romance stories help us become our best selves?

BOOK CLUB
DISCUSSION GUIDE

Nola is available for in-person and zoom appearances.
with your Book Club. For information and availability,
please write: nola@nolasaintjames.com.

If We Could Talk to the Animals ...

In *Midnight Miracle*, Grace learns about the legend that animals can talk in the human tongue at midnight on Christmas Eve. She begins to hope that the animals she loves and cares for, Blackie, the stallion, Bronwyn, the mare, Grey, her old pony and Balthazar, the donkey, can tell her the name of her true love.

Grace learns, when she goes to the stable at midnight on Christmas Eve, that although the animals can talk, they may not be able or willing to tell her what she wants to know. However, she experiences new facets of their personalities. The stories that they share about her parents helps to help soften her grief at their loss.

We know that animals speak to and understand one another. Have you ever felt that an animal that you are close to was about to speak to you? What would its voice sound like? How would its way of expressing itself be different from human speech? What would an animal you love want to say to you? What would you hope it would say? Would being able to talk directly to a beloved animal change your relationship to it?

Why Bother to Find Out the Initials of One's Fated Mate?

Grace has a dowry and she is the daughter of a viscount. However, as an orphan and a young woman, she is at the mercy of her male trustees. She has no money of her own and no options with respect to determining her own future. She hopes that by learning the initials of her fated love, she can recognize him and marry him quickly before her trustees marry her off to a man of their choice.

Grace performs the apple peel divination ritual to determine the letters of the name of her intended husband. This is a real tradition whose roots are lost in the mists of the ages. There are many other types of rituals that women have used throughout the ages — and even today — to try to predict their marital future. Why would women go to such lengths to determine who they are fated to marry?

Throughout history, and even today in many parts of the world, a woman's future is determined by her ability to marry and leave her parents' home. For many women, their only opportunity for some level of independence as an adult, is to find a husband who will support her and any children they may have.

From the time girls are very young, they are groomed and socialized to be wives and mothers. The option for a woman to be single, self-supporting and independent, is only available to women who live in first world countries and who are from families that have some financial stability or upward mobility. Therefore, from an early age, young girls understand that the question of "who will I marry" is of the utmost importance to their future happiness. Any type of ritual that promises to open a window into this mystery is of interest.

Over the last 200 years, how have women's ability to determine their own choices changed? What forces in society today restrict women's choices for their futures? What factors support women's opportunities? How can women claim their lives and live as they choose?

Is the Utopian Dream of the Hungry Dragon a Vision That Can Be Realized?

The fable of the Hungry Dragon is about an idealized community in which everyone lives in harmony. When everyone supports everyone else, good times are magnified, and difficulties are shared and minimized. Everyone lives a happy life.

Into this perfect world comes a force that is out of harmony, as embodied by the wealthy lord and lady and their soldiers. They judge the town and the tavern by the standards of their world. The lord and lady find the town so unworthy of their notice that they order it destroyed. It is only through the magical power of the Hungry Dragon that the town is saved.

In typical fashion, after the village is spared, the villagers gather together to commemorate this memorable event so that their descendants will never forget. It is their intention that the life that they have built, of cooperation and love for one another, will be passed on from generation to generation.

The first mention of a utopian community in Western Literature is found in the first chapters of the biblical book of Genesis. God creates a perfect world for plants and animals, including humans, in which all can exist in peace and humans are immortal. It's kind of like a snow globe. Ultimately, the Garden of Eden doesn't work for humans, and they are placed on earth as we know it, to life, and to die.

Ever since then, we humans have been trying to create other utopias. Because humans are imperfect, utopian societies tend to ultimately fail. However, the human wish for a perfected world, where all is in balance and all people have equally good lives, is a powerful motivator for social change.

If you had the ability to create a utopian community, what would it look like? Who would be able to join? What kind of rules would you put in place? How would you guarantee its continuity? What problems do you think you would face?

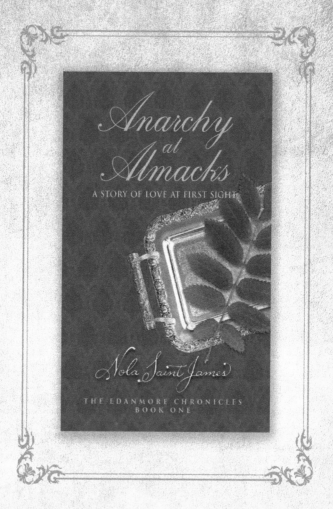

**Have you read *Anarchy at Almacks:
A Story of Love at First Sight*?**

Now available on Amazon, B&N.com
and on Kindle Unlimited.

PROLOGUE

London, the beginning of the Season
The Ton Reporter, **Thursday, April 5, 1804**

*If last night's riot at Almacks is any indication, the Season of
1804 is going to prove to be of unprecedented interest. More blood
was spilled on the hallowed floors of London's most exclusive meeting
place for single ladies and gentlemen than one might find on the
ground trod by two champion bare-knuckle boxers.*

*Aristocratic noses were bloodied and broken as the ton's Pinks
and Corinthians fought their way across the dance floor toward the
evening's main attraction — three lovely, flame-haired sisters from
the idyllic isle of Edanmore. The breathtaking Higbee sisters — the
Misses Rowan, 22, Willow, 20 and Ivy,
18 — seemed unperturbed by the pandemonium that resulted from
their mere entrance into Almacks hallowed halls. Anyone seeing them
together might have cautioned their parents to bring them out one at
time. Any one of them would be the Diamond of her season! But put
them all together? A riot at Almacks may only be the first of such events
during this season. Indeed, Parliament may well have to pass a law
prohibiting the three young ladies from appearing together in public, in
order to keep the peace!*

*As the melee increased in volume, combativeness, the crunching
of bones and the flowing of blood, other young ladies, fresh from the
country, fainted dead away. Virile young men fighting to stake their
claim on the ton's newest arrivals, was unique in the history of that
hallowed hall.*

—S. J. ROBERTS, SOCIETY REPORTER

Almacks — Wednesday, April 4, 1804.

CHAPTER ONE
Mayhem at Almacks

*It is the duty of the eldest sister to set an example for the sisters
who come after her. She should not attempt to be perfect or to mimic
perfection. She should just try to do her best. She should always
be honest with her sisters about her missteps. By her honesty, they
will learn that life is not about our triumphs, but about how we
manage our failures. By her good example, when her sisters
make their own mistakes, they will know that it is possible to pick
oneself up and move on.*

— Lady X's Admonitions to Young Women (Third Edition, 1802)

Almacks Assembly Rooms
Wednesday, April 4, 1804 – The night before

"Great God in Heaven! Who?" Lord Maximillian Francis
Browning, Max to his friends, couldn't say another word. He
grabbed the shoulders of his boon companion, Lord Richard Grey
Birmingham, and forcefully spun him around to face the entranceway
to Almacks ballroom. It was the first Wednesday of the Season, and
the room was buzzing in the anticipation of a new crop of young

ladies making their come outs.

Both men gazed in wonder at a trio of stunning, red-haired young ladies who had just entered Almacks' hallowed halls. They were chaperoned by a distinguished older couple, obviously their parents.

"Good Lord!" cried Grey. "I heard about the Higbee sisters from my mother, but I never imagined that they looked like that."

"The one with the darkest red hair?"

"That's Miss Rowan Higbee, the eldest sister," said a woman's voice behind him.

Max turned and looked into the kind, blue eyes of his mother's dearest friend, Lady Saxby.

"I met their mother one summer when I spent some time on Edanmore Island. All the young women are lovely."

At just that moment, the sister with the darkest red hair, Miss Rowan, caught Max's dark brown eyes. Her shining sapphire-blue eyes seemed to pierce his soul. Max felt as though he had stopped breathing. From somewhere deep within, he heard a voice shout, "It is she!"

Then, "Mine!"

Without realizing it, Max began to move towards the woman he now thought of as his Rowan. The voice prodded him, "Go. Go to her. This is really and truly love!"

"This is it," thought Max as he began to move toward his soon-to-be wife. He was somewhat taller than most of the men in the ballroom and could keep Rowan in sight as he moved across the room. Grey, an inch shorter, with the muscular build of a man who regularly worked the land, walked slightly ahead of him. The roiling mass of humanity parted before them. As they made their way toward the entrance, Lady Sefton, one of the patronesses of Almacks, came forward to greet the family, all smiles.

"Have you ever?" asked Max.

"Never!" said Grey.

Had Max been less entranced, he would have realized he was not the only man making his way in the direction of the three young women. It was as if they were magnets to whom the gentlemen in the room were irresistibly attracted.

As the mass of men moved forward, they began jostling one another. Because Almacks did not serve spirits, some of the men had imbibed heavily before appearing at the assembly hall. In their alcohol-fueled haze, they began to object to being hindered from reaching the three young beauties.

Unexpected collisions began to occur. Voices were raised. More deliberate shoving commenced. Fists began to fly. A few noses were broken. Blood began to flow. Before anyone could stop it, a full-scale riot had broken out. Some young ladies fainted. Others shrieked in alarm. A few women were secretly thrilled!

The impact of these lovely ladies was felt not only by the young bucks! The venerable Duke of B — well into his eighth decade, was seen slowly shuffling to their side. Thankfully, because of his exalted status in the ton, everyone gave him a wide berth. Several of the dowagers present surrounded him to assure that he was not jostled.

Lady Sefton and several other patronesses surrounded the family and whisked them away to a private room where they could wait for their carriage.

The Ton Reporter, **The Fashion Page**
Thursday, April 5, 1804

The riot at Almacks last night (see S. J. Roberts news report) might not have occurred had not the family of the Baron Edanmore been accepted as a client of the renowned modiste, Madame Celeste Laval. The three flame-haired sisters were dressed in ensembles crafted by this unparalleled gift to London's world of fashion.

Miss Rowan Higbee was dressed in a creation — one cannot call it simply a gown — of royal-blue silk with an overlay of tissue-thin white lace embellished with tiny diamonds. To say she was breathtaking would be a gross understatement. Tiny diamond pins could be seen shyly peeking out of her curls, which were arranged in a cluster all over her head. Around her neck, she wore a perfectly spherical solitary pearl as big as a quail's egg, suspended on a silver chain so delicate that it seemed as though the pearl hovered in thin air above her décolletage. Would it fall? The suspense was heart-stopping!

Smaller pearls, equally perfect, were suspended from the lady's delicate ear lobes. They moved with her every step, seeming to be in communion with her very breath. Taken all together, Miss Higbee seemed like nothing less than the essence of twilight that had drifted into the room bringing the moon and stars with her. What is more, she seemed completely unconscious of the fact that she put the angels to shame.

Miss Willow, who is the tallest of the three sisters, has the lightest red hair, an arresting pale orange gold that is straight and extremely silky. She wore it pulled back and woven into an elaborate knot high on the back of her head.

Her gown was the compelling green of an ancient-growth forest, but with a sheen that made it seem as though the gown was constantly changing colors. The blue of a clear morning sky, the darker blue/grey of early evening and a hint of red at sundown constantly swirled around her. The dress featured a flowing train that hung from Miss Willow's shoulders.

To complement her ensemble, she wore a delicate gold net collar that hugged her neck and then descended to just above the top of her bodice. It was studded with emeralds, sapphires and rubies. In her ears, she wore emerald stud earrings. Rather than making her seem like a fabulously wealthy heiress — which she may or may not be, the combination of gown and jewels seemed to enhance an innate "fey" quality that seems to be a natural and unconscious part of her being.

Miss Ivy, the youngest of the three sisters at just 18, is Venus in miniature. She is all carrot-red curls, luminous green eyes, skin the color of wave foam and generous curves perfectly suited to her

diminutive proportions. The lady exudes an air of kindness, and
her eyes seem to notice everything around her. When she became
aware of the fracas, her immediate and generous impulse was to
rush to the aid of the fallen men. She was gently restrained by her
mother, who needed only to place her hand gently on her daughter's
shoulder to prevent the girl's movement.

This lovely young woman was dressed in white, which is de
rigueur for the youngest of young ladies making their come out. To
say it was a "white dress" would be to say that a glorious sunrise is
just the sun coming up.

Madame Laval's true genius is that her fashions, in their
restraint, permit the personality of the wearer to shine through.
It wouldn't surprise this writer at all if there is not some sorcery
involved. In the case of Miss Ivy, Madame's creation highlighted
the young lady's natural sweetness and modesty, while gently
suggesting that she is so much more.

Miss Ivy wore a simple, white-silk sheath that tastefully
displayed her assets to best advantage. The scalloped neckline was
higher than usual but in covering up it also emphasized Miss Ivy's
charms. The short, slightly puffed sleeves were slashed and inset
with thin strips of gold velvet. The pleats at the back of her dress
were also lined with the same material.

Her lovely carrot-red curls were studded with small emerald
pins. Around her neck, she wore a simple circlet of fire opals
with matching stones in her ears. To call that necklace simple is
a misnomer. It was as though all the good spirits residing on the
idyllic island of Edanmore were surrounding her with their love and
joy. In all, Miss Ivy was the ideal presentation of all that a young
lady making her debut should be.

Our sources tell us that a debut ball for the three sisters is
being planned for some time later this season. It will take place
at Edanmore House, which has recently been reNovoted and
decorated by the baron's fourth son, noted architect, Mr. Brian

Higbee, assisted by his talented wife, the daughter of the Comte de Lorainne. It is said that the baron spared no expense in the decoration and furnishing of the house. In addition, the installation of the newest conveniences reportedly includes the piping of heated water to bathing rooms on every floor.

A word to the young men of the ton planning to attend Almacks next Wednesday: "Keep a sober head!" The impact of the Flame Sisters may, in time, lessen as we mere mortals are exposed to their allure. In the meantime, maintaining one's faculties is strongly advised.

Illustrations of the ensembles created by Madame Laval for the Flame Sisters for their first appearance at Almacks can be found below this article. We thank Madame for supplying these with the permission of Baron Edanmore.

What spectacle will the Flame Sisters ignite in the weeks ahead?

No one knew it then, but what was later to be remembered as "The Season of the Flame Sisters" had just begun.

Mincemeat Tarts
for Any Season

Mincemeat tarts are a traditional Christmas treat because of their warming spices, (think pumpkin pie,) alcoholic content and the use of preserved fruits. Hundreds of years ago, meat and suet were added to the fruit mixture. Today, most mincemeat tarts are completely meat-free and have a delicious filling of spiced fresh and dried fruits. The pastry dough can be made with butter or vegan butter substitutes, so the tarts can easily be vegan friendly.

While it is perfectly fine to make these tarts from scratch, it is extremely easy to make quick and delicious mincemeat tarts with prepared pie dough and excellent commercially available mincemeat fillings. If you wish to bake "from scratch," there are many mincemeat tart and pie recipes on the internet. This is a time saving version.

Mrs. Beaton's and Nola's Quick and Easy Mincemeat Tarts

Ingredients

- 1 package of prepared pie dough
  (not a shell unless you are baking a pie)
  vegan pie dough if preferred

- 1 jar of prepared mincemeat filling
  (see brand suggestions below)
  All are labeled vegan or are vegan-friendly

- 1 large egg lightly beaten with 1 tablespoon water
  (for egg wash)
  For vegans, substitute maple syrup, almond milk
  or Just Egg.

- Good quality sweet butter or good quality sweet
  vegan butter

- 2 tablespoons powdered sugar for sifting onto
  the top of the tarts

- Flour for work surface

Equipment

1 muffin pan. This recipe is based on a standard muffin pan. One can also use mini muffin pans for bite-sized mincemeat tartlets.

1 circular pastry cutter – 3.5" round

1 star pastry cutter – 2 to 2/1/4" – smaller if using mini pans

Rolling pin.

Instructions

1   Preheat oven to 400 degrees F.
2   Lightly brush the wells and sides of a muffin pan with butter.

3   Divide the pie dough into 2 equal parts. Roll each into a ball, flatten each ball slightly into a disk, wrap them in plastic wrap, and refrigerate until ready to use. Use one ball at a time, reserving the rest of the dough in the refrigerator.

4   Place 1 disk of dough onto a floured work surface. Working from the center out, roll the dough out to a rectangle about 11" to 12" by 16" to 18".

5   To make the tarts in a regular muffin pan, you will need (16) 3.5" circles and (16) 2- 2 ¼" stars for topping the tarts. Cut out as many as you can from each piece of rolled dough. Gather the dough scraps, re-roll the dough and cut out more if needed.

6   Gently press each circle of dough into a muffin well in a muffin pan. Make sure the dough is not too thick and not too thin. Too thick, and you won't have enough filling; too thin and the pastry will collapse when you try to eat the tart.

7   Use a fork to poke a few holes in the bottom crust of each tart.

8   Fill each dough circle about 3/4 full of the mincemeat filling (about 2 tablespoons per tart), making sure the filling is compact and there are no air bubbles.

9   Place 1 star on top of each tart. Lightly brush each star with egg wash or egg wash substitute.

10   Bake until the crusts are golden brown — about 20 to 22 minutes.

11   Let them cool for 15 minutes in the tray before removing. Run a paring knife around the outside of the tart if necessary to help release the tarts from the muffin pan.

12   Lightly dust each tart with the powdered sugar by putting the sugar in a small wire mesh strainer and shaking it over each tart. Use a spoon to help push the sugar through, if necessary.

Notes

Storage: You can store mince tarts in an airtight container in the refrigerator for up to 1 week.

To reheat, preheat the oven to 350F, put the tarts on a baking tray, and bake until warm, about 5 to 8 minutes. For a fast reheat, put on a microwave plate and heat through for 30-60 seconds.

Freezer-Friendly: To freeze these tarts, let them cool to room temperature. Then store in an airtight container, separated by pieces of parchment paper. They will stay fresh-tasting for about 3 months.

A Recipe for Homemade Mincemeat Filling

Ingredients

- teaspoon each of ground cinnamon, ground cloves, ground ginger, ground nutmeg and ground allspice.

   Or
- 5 teaspoons of pumpkin pie spice mix – same spices!

Mincemeat:

- 1 large green apple, peeled and finely chopped
- 1 ¼ cups sultana raisins (white raisins)
- 1 ⅛ cups white sugar (or combine ½ and ½ with brown sugar)
- ½ cup dried currants
- ½ cup raisins
- ½ cup sweet butter or sweet vegan butter
- ½ cup chopped almonds (or walnuts or a mix of these)
- 1 ½ tablespoons grated orange zest (or chopped candied orange or lemon peel)
- 1 teaspoon of cinnamon
- 1 cup brandy - For a non-alcoholic alternative, cook the alcohol out of the brandy or substitute orange juice.

Directions

1. Immerse two clean, 12-ounce jars in simmering water until mincemeat is ready. Wash new, unused lids and rings in warm soapy water.
2. To prepare the mincemeat:
   - Combine apple, sultanas, sugar, currants, raisins, and butter in a saucepan.
   - Cook over low heat and stir gently until butter has melted.
   - Stir in chopped almonds, orange zest/peel 1 teaspoon mixed spice, and cinnamon.
   - Bring mixture to a simmer and cook, stirring occasionally, 5 to 10 minutes.
   - Remove from heat and set mincemeat aside to cool for 30 minutes.
   - When cool, stir in brandy. Spoon into sterilized jars.
3. Refrigerate. The mixture can stay in the refrigerator for about a month.
4. Let the mincemeat age in the refrigerator for at least 24 hours before using.
5. Mincemeat filling can be frozen in an airtight container for up to 12 months to extend its shelf life. When freezing, it's important to leave some space in the container because the filling will expand slightly.

Serving Suggestions for Mincemeat

Mincemeat filling is delicious over vanilla ice cream and with plain or vanilla yogurt. It can also be used as a fruit filling for pancakes and served over pound cake or sponge cake and topped with whipped cream or custard.

Some quality prepared mincemeat brands

Note: None of these brands uses fructose as a primary ingredient and all are vegan-friendly.

Tiptree Mincemeat

Ingredients: Vine Fruits, Sugar, Apples, Cider, Rapeseed Oil, Citrus Peel, Brandy, Acetic Acid, Mixed Spice. Gluten free, made in a nut free factory, suitable for vegetarians and vegans.

The Wilkin family has been farming in Tiptree, Essex, since 1757, and making quality preserves since 1885. The majority of the fruit used in Tiptree jars are grown on their own farm, ensuring fruit is hand-picked with care at the most optimal time.

Robertson's Mincemeat

A classic mincemeat recipe from Scotland.
Ingredients: Sugar, Apples (26%), Vine Fruit (26%) (Sultanas, Raisins, Currants), Candied Mixed Citrus Peel (4%) (Glucose-Fructose Syrup, Orange Peel, Sugar, Lemon Peel), Vegetable Suet (Palm Oil, Sunflower Oil), Treacle, Preservative: Acetic Acid; Mixed Spice, Acidity Regulator: Citric Acid.

Foods Of Athenry Festively Fruity Mince Meat

Gluten, Wheat, Dairy, Egg and Milk Free.
82% fruit & nut content; and a fat content of under 4% per 100g.
Gluten, wheat, dairy & egg free. Vegan.

Ingredients:

Mincemeat: sultanas, sugar, raisins, apple, fresh grated carrot, dates, mixed citrus peel, currants, glacé cherries, vegetable suet, brandy, cider, sherry, almonds, walnuts, mixed spice, lemon juice, cinnamon, acidity regulator: acetic acid, plain caramel, orange rind oil, lemon rind oil. glace cherries contains (cherries, sugar, glucose-fructose syrup, acidity regulator: citric acid, colour: anthocyanin) mixed citrus peel contains (orange & lemon peel, glucose-fructose syrup, acidity regulator: citric acid). vegetable suet contains (sustainable palm oil, sunflower oil, rice flour).

For a wonderful recipe for a traditional Christmas Cake, visit Nola's website – nolasaintjames.com

Regency Romance Words and Phrases

Here are five Regency-specific words and phrases used in this story. For an expanded list, please visit nolasaintjames.com

Rom, Romany (page 4)

The term **Rom** or **Romany** refers to itinerate groups of people who were traditionally called gypsies. One such group originated in South Asia and dispersed across Europe and North and South America. Their native language is Romani, which is related to Hindi.

In the United Kingdom, in data collection, the term Gypsies includes such specific groups as English Gypsies, Scottish Gypsies (sometimes referred to as Travelers,) Welsh Gypsies and other Romany groups. Irish Travelers have specific Irish roots. More recently, the general term Roma is associated with itinerant recent migrants from Central and Eastern Europe.

In the English language (according to the Oxford English Dictionary), Rom is a noun (with the plural Romá or Roms) and an adjective, while Romany is also a noun (with the plural Romanies) and an adjective. Both Rom and Romany have been in use in English since the 19th century as an alternative for Gypsy.

Playing Ducks and Drakes (page 14)

This saying is thought to go back to the late 16th century. While the precise origin is unclear, it is thought to refer to the way in which ducks act in the water — taking off from a pond with a lot of flapping of wings, or making rings when splashing, or bobbing their heads. It has come to have the meaning of handling something recklessly or with possible ill intent, or to squander resources.

Ashmead's Kernel apples (page 30)

This is a type of green apple which originated in England in the 1700's. Although not particularly attractive, it has a unique flavor that is reminiscent of pear. This has made it a popular eating apple. Ashmead's Kernel is very versatile. It is delicious when eaten raw, but it can also be cooked with good results. It produces excellent juice and hard cider.

Curry (page 64)

This term, when used in relation to horses, has nothing to do with cooking!

The word *curry* is derived from the French word *correirer* — to put in order, to prepare or arrange. In English, this term has been around for about 800 years. It refers to rubbing down or grooming a horse. To do this, one uses a *curry comb*. When currying a horse, one is rearranging the horse's hair into a more ideal direction. Thus the connection to the French word.

To Marry Over the Anvil (page 99)

In 1754, in England, a new marriage law was passed that prohibited young people under 21 to marry without their parents' or guardian's consent. This law did not apply to Scotland. In Scotland, anyone over the age of 15 could enter into marriage as long as they were not closely related to the other person and were not in a committed relationship with someone else. The marriage could take place in private or public with or without witnesses anywhere in Scotland.

Gretna Green, which is in the southern council area of Dumfries and Galloway, is the closest town in Scotland adjacent to the English border. In the 1770's, a toll road was built which ran through the town. This made it even more accessible to the English border. Gretna quickly became the destination for eloping couples.

In Scotland, it was not necessary, as it was in England, to have a priest officiate at a marriage. The most senior and respected craftsman in most villages was the village blacksmith. The Blacksmith's Forge at Gretna Green soon became the traditional place to marry. To "seal" the marriage, the blacksmith would strike his anvil. This custom led to the Gretna blacksmiths becoming known as 'anvil priests.' It is still possible to marry in Gretna Green over the anvil. Please note, even in the 18th and 19th century, the price of a wedding was not cheap. Today modern prices prevail.

Want to Read More About Christmas Traditions and Legends?

I really enjoyed these books. I hope you will too.

 The Animals Speak: A Christmas Eve Legend, Marion Dane Bauer, Beaming Books, 2021. Intended for children 3 -8, this charming story tells of the songs that animals sing at the birth of the child in the manger. Beautifully illustrated by Brittany Baugus.

 The Night the Animals Talked, Patricia Barry Rumble, Kimberly Noel Smith, illustrator, Playitstore Publishing, 2012. This award-winning juvenile novel is about a multi-generational family getting ready to put on a play – The Night the Animals Talked – in their front yard. A sudden disaster upsets the family and interferes with their Christmas preparations. Will there be a happy ending?

 Linda Goodman's Love Signs: New Edition of the Classic Astrology Book on Love: Unlock Your True Love Match, Linda Goodman, Bluebird, 2022. An update of the classic 1979 edition. Can a Capricorn find love with a Sagittarius? This is a complete astrological guide to personal relationships, offering compelling insight and advice for every zodiac sign — and the compatibility of every possible pairing. Lively, entertaining and informative, written by the world-famous astrologer.

Winter Tales, Dawn Casey, Zanna Goldhawk, illustrator, Templar Publishing, 2020. A lovely book of winter folk tales from all over the world - from North America to Siberia, Scotland, France, Russia and Norway. Stay warm and toasty as you travel the world on a Christmas adventure.

 The Secret History of Christmas Baking: Recipes & Stories from Tomb Offerings to Gingerbread Boys, Linda Raedisch, Llewellyn Publications, 2023. This charming book features some of the world's most iconic Christmas recipes. They are interspersed with stories of sailors, saints, tomb raiders, and artisans. Learn the secret history of some of the West's most delectable Christmas treats.

 The Man Who Invented Christmas: How Charles Dickens's A Christmas Carol Rescued His Career and Revived Our Holiday Spirits, Les Standiford, Deckle Edge, 2008. Learn how a debt-ridden and dispirited Charles Dickens self-published a small tale to raise money to pay his creditors and in the process planted the seeds for our modern celebration of Christmas! Travel back to Victorian England for an infusion of warmth, wit, and Christmas cheer.

What did you think of
Midnight Miracle?

If you enjoyed this book,
please leave a review on Amazon.com.
Thank you so much.
Every review is a tremendous help!

WRITE TO US AT
NOLA@NOLASAINTJAMES.COM

SIGN UP FOR OUR
NEWSLETTER AT NOLASAINTJAMES.COM